THE
HOUSE
OF
BLUE
LEAVES

ALSO BY *John Guare*

Cop Out, Muzeeka,
and Home Fires

Seated, left to right: Katherine Helmond (Bananas Shaughnessy); Warren Lyons, coproducer; Faith Geer, publicist; Betty Ann Besch, coproducer; William Atherton (Ronnie Shaughnessy); Frank Converse (Billy Einhorn); Margaret Linn (Corrinna Stroller); Anne Meara (Bunny Flingus); Kay Michaels (the Second Nun); Harold Gould (Artie Shaughnessy); Rita Karin (the Head Nun). *Standing, left to right:* Alix Elias (the Little Nun); John Guare; Mel Shapiro, director; Carl Hunt (the White Man); Thomas Flynn (the M.P.); Charles Briggs, stage manager.

THE
HOUSE
OF

a play by
JOHN GUARE

BLUE
LEAVES

NEW YORK   *The Viking Press*

First published in 1972 in a hardbound and paperbound edition by
The Viking Press, Inc.
625 Madison Avenue, New York, N.Y. 10022

Published simultaneously in Canada by
The Macmillan Company of Canada Limited

SBN 670-38018-0 (hardbound)
    670-00353-0 (paperbound)

Library of Congress catalog card number: 70-183513

Photographs by Martha Swope

Printed in U.S.A. by The Colonial Press Inc.

Foreword

The House of Blue Leaves takes place in Sunnyside, Queens, one of the five boroughs of New York City. You have to understand Queens. It was never a borough with its own identity like Brooklyn that people clapped for on quiz shows if you said you came from there. Brooklyn had been a city before it became part of New York, so it always had its own identity. And the Bronx originally had been Jacob Bronck's farm, which at least gives it something personal, and Staten Island is out there on the way to the sea, and, of course, Manhattan is what people mean when they say New York.

Queens was built in the twenties in that flush of optimism as a bedroom community for people on their way up who worked in Manhattan but wanted to pretend they had the better things in life until the inevitable break came and they could make the official move to the Scarsdales and the Ryes and the Greenwiches of their dreams, the pay-off that was the birthright of every American. Queens named its communities Forest Hills, Kew Gardens, Elmhurst, Woodside, Sunnyside, Jackson Heights, Corona, Astoria (after the Astors, of all people). The builders built the apartment houses in mock Tudor or Gothic or Colonial and then named them The Chateau, The El Dorado, Linsley Hall, The Alhambra. We lived first in The East Gate, then moved to The West Gate, then to Hampton Court. And the lobbies had Chippendale furniture and Aztec fireplaces, and the elevators had roman numerals on the buttons.

And in the twenties and thirties and forties you'd move there and move out as soon as you could. Your young married days were over, the promotions came. The ads in the magazines were right. Hallelujah. Queens: a comfortable rest stop, a pleasant rung on the ladder of success, a promise we were promised in some secret dream. And isn't Manhattan, each day the skyline growing denser and more crenelated, always looming up there in the distance? The elevated subway, the Flushing line, zooms to it, only fourteen minutes from Grand Central Station. Everything you could want you'd find right there in Queens. But the young marrieds become old marrieds, and the children come, but the promotions, the breaks, don't, and you're still there in your bedroom community, your life over the bridge in Manhattan, and the fourteen-minute ride becomes longer every day. Why didn't I get the breaks? I'm right here in the heart of the action, in the bedroom community of the heart of the action, and I live in the El Dorado Apartments and the main street of Jackson Heights has Tudor-topped buildings with pizza slices for sale beneath them and discount radios and discount drugs and discount records and the Chippendale-paneled elevator in my apartment is all carved up with Love To Fuck that no amount of polishing can ever erase. And why do my dreams, which should be the best part of me, why do my dreams, my wants, constantly humiliate me? Why don't I get the breaks? What happened? I'm hip. I'm hep. I'm a New Yorker. The heart of the action. Just a subway ride to the heart of the action. I want to be part of that skyline. I want to blend into those lights. Hey, dreams, I dreamed you. I'm not something you curb a dog for. New York is where it all is. So why aren't I here? When I was a kid, I wanted to come from Iowa, from New Mexico, to make the final break and leave, say, the flatness of Nebraska and get on that Greyhound and get off that Greyhound at Port Authority and you wave your cardboard suitcase at the sky: I'll Lick You Yet. How do you run away to your dreams when you're already there? I never wanted to be any place in my life but New York. How do you get there when you're there? Fourteen minutes on the Flushing line is a very long distance. And I guess that's what this play is about more than anything else: humiliation. Everyone in the play is constantly being humiliated by their dreams, their loves, their wants, their best parts. People have criticized the play for being cruel or unfeeling. I don't think any play from the Oresteia on down has ever reached the cruelty of the smallest moments in our lives, what we have done to others, what others have done to us. I'm not interested so much in how people survive as in how they avoid humiliation. Chekhov says we must never humiliate one another, and I think avoiding humiliation is the core of tragedy and comedy and probably of our lives.

This is how the play got written: I went to Saint Joan of Arc Grammar School in Jackson Heights, Queens, from 1944 to 1952 (wildly pre-Berrigan years). The nuns would say, If only we could get to Rome, to have His Holiness touch us, just to see Him, capital H, the Vicar of Christ on Earth—Vicar, V.I.C.A.R., Vicar, in true spelling-bee style. Oh, dear God, help me get to Rome, the capital of Italy, and go to that special little country in the heart of the capital—V.A.T.I.C.A.N.C.I.T.Y.—and touch the Pope. No sisters ever yearned for Moscow the way those sisters and their pupils yearned for Rome. And in 1965 I finally got to Rome. Sister Carmela! Do you hear me? I got here! It's a new Pope, but they're all the same. Sister Benedict! I'm here! And I looked at the Rome papers, and there on the front page was a picture of the Pope. On Queens Boulevard. I got to Rome on the day a Pope left the Vatican to come to New York for the first time to plead to the United Nations for peace in the world on October 4, 1965. He passed through Queens, because you have to on the way from Kennedy Airport to Manhattan. Like the Borough of Queens itself, that's how much effect the Pope's pleas for peace had. The Pope's no loser. Neither is Artie Shaughnessy, whom *The House of Blue Leaves* is about. They both have big dreams. Lots of possibilities. The Pope's just into more real estate.

My parents wrote me about that day that the Pope came to New York and how thrilled they were, and the letter caught up with me in Cairo because I was hitching from Paris to the Sudan. And I started thinking about my parents and me and why was I in Egypt and what was I doing with my life and what were they doing with theirs, and that's how plays get started. The play is autobiographical in the sense that everything in the play happened in one way or another over a period of years, and some of it happened in dreams and some of it could have happened and some of it, luckily, never happened. But it's autobiographical all the same. My father worked for the New York Stock Exchange, but he called it a zoo and Artie in the play is a zoo-keeper. The Billy in the play is my mother's brother, Billy, a monstrous man who was head of casting at MGM from the thirties through the fifties. The Huckleberry Finn episode that begins Act Two is an exact word-for-word reportage of what happened between Billy and me at our first meeting. The play is a blur of many years that pulled together under the umbrella of the Pope's visit.

In 1966 I wrote the first act of the play, and, like some bizarre revenge or disapproval, on the day I finished it my father died. The first act was performed at the O'Neill Theatre Center in Waterford, Connecticut, and I played Artie. The second act came in a rush after that and all the events in that first draft are the same as you'll find in this version. But in 1966 the steam, the impetus for the play, had gone. I wrote another draft of the second act. Another. A fourth. A fifth. A sixth. A director I had been working with was leading the play into abysmal naturalistic areas with all the traps that a set with a kitchen sink in it can have. I was lost on the play until 1969 in London, when one night at the National Theatre I saw Laurence Olivier do *Dance of Death* and the next night, still reeling from it, saw him in Charon's production of *A Flea in Her Ear*. The savage intensity of the first blended into the maniacal intensity of the second, and somewhere in my head *Dance of Death* became the same play as *A Flea in Her Ear*. Why shouldn't Strindberg and Feydeau get married, at least live together, and *The House of Blue Leaves* be their child? For years my two favorite shows had been *Gypsy* and *The Homecoming*. I think the only playwrighting rule is that you have to learn your craft so that you can put on stage plays you would like to see. So I threw away all the second acts of the play, started in again, and, for the first time, understood what I wanted.

Before I was born, just before, my father wrote a song for my mother:

> A stranger's coming to our house.
> I hope he likes us.
> I hope he stays.
> I hope he doesn't go away.

I liked them, loved them, stayed too long, and didn't go away. This play is for them.

—JOHN GUARE

New York, 1971

CHARACTERS

Artie Shaughnessy
Ronnie Shaughnessy
Bunny Flingus
Bananas Shaughnessy
Corrinna Stroller
Billy Einhorn
Three nuns
A military policeman
The white man

SCENE

A cold apartment in Sunnyside, Queens,
New York City.

TIME

October 4, 1965

Music and lyrics by John Guare

Warren Lyons and Betty Ann Besch presented *The House of Blue Leaves* in New York City, opening February 10, 1970, at the Truck and Warehouse Theatre. The production was directed by Mel Shapiro.

Cast

ARTIE SHAUGHNESSY	*Harold Gould*
RONNIE SHAUGHNESSY	*William Atherton*
BUNNY FLINGUS	*Anne Meara*
BANANAS SHAUGHNESSY	*Katherine Helmond*
CORRINNA STROLLER	*Margaret Linn*
BILLY EINHORN	*Frank Converse*
THE HEAD NUN	*Rita Karin*
THE SECOND NUN	*Kay Michaels*
THE LITTLE NUN	*Alix Elias*
THE M.P.	*Thomas Flynn*
THE WHITE MAN	*Carl Hunt*

Karl Eigsti designed the settings. Jane Greenwood designed the costumes. John Tedesco designed the lighting. Michael Eisner of ABC-TV supplied the TV footage of the Pope's visit.

A staged reading of the first act was performed in August 1966 at the Eugene O'Neill Playwrights Conference, Waterford, Connecticut, with Kay Michaels as Bananas, Peggy Pope as Bunny, and John Guare as Artie.

THE
HOUSE
OF
BLUE
LEAVES

Prologue

The stage of the El Dorado Bar & Grill.

While the house lights are still on, and the audience is still being seated, ARTIE SHAUGHNESSY *comes on stage through the curtains, bows, and sits at the upright piano in front of the curtain. He is forty-five years old. He carries sheet music and an opened bottle of beer. He scowls into the wings and then smiles broadly out front.*

ARTIE, *out front; nervous:* My name is Artie Shaughnessy and I'm going to sing you songs I wrote. I wrote all these songs. Words and the music. Could I have some quiet, please? *Sings brightly:*

> Back together again,
> Back together again.
> Since we split up
> The skies we lit up
> Looked all bit up
> Like Fido chewed them,
> But they're back together again.
> You can say you knew us when
> We were together;
> Now we're apart,
> Thunder and lightning's
> Back in my heart,
> And that's the weather to be
> When you're back together with me.

Into the wings: Could you please turn the lights down? A spotlight on me? You promised me a spotlight.

Out front: I got a ballad I'm singing and you promised me a blue spotlight.

The house lights remain on. People are still finding their seats.

ARTIE—*plunges on into a ballad; sentimentally:*

> I'm looking for Something,
> I've searched everywhere,

I'm looking for something
And just when I'm there,
Whenever I'm near it
I can see it and hear it,
I'm almost upon it,
Then it's gone.
It seems I'm looking for Something
But what can it be?
I just need a Someone
To hold close to me.
I'll tell you a secret,
Please keep it entre nous,
That Someone
I thought it was you.

Out front: Could you please take your seats and listen? I'm going to sing you a song I wrote at work today and I hope you like it as much as I do. *Plays and sings:*

Where is the devil in Evelyn?
What's it doing in Angela's eyes?
Evelyn is heavenly,
Angela's in a devil's disguise.
I know about the sin in Cynthia
And the hell in Helen of Troy,
But where is the devil in Evelyn?
What's it doing in Angela's eyes?

Oh boy!
What's it doing in Angela's eyes?

He leaps up from the piano with his sheet music and beer, bows to the audience. Waits for applause. Bows. Waits. Looks. Runs off stage.
House lights go down.

Artie Shaughnessy

Act

One

Curtain up.

The living room of a shabby apartment in Sunnyside, Queens. The room is filled with many lamps and pictures of movie stars and jungle animals.

Upstage center is a bay window, the only window in the room. Across the opening of the bay is a crisscross-barred folding gate of the kind jewelers draw across the front of their stores at night. Outside the window is a fire escape. A small window in the side of the bay is close enough to the gate to be opened or closed by reaching through the bars.

It's late at night and a street lamp beams some light into this dark place through the barred window.

A piano near the window is covered with hundreds of pieces of sheet music and manuscript paper and beer bottles. A jacket, shirt, and pants—the green uniform of a city employee—are draped over the end of the piano nearest the window.

We can see ARTIE *asleep on the couch, zipped tightly into a sleeping bag, snoring fitfully and mumbling:* "Pope Ronnie. Pope Ronnie. Pope Ronald the First. Pope Ronald."

We can see a pullman kitchen with its doors open far stage right.

Three other doors in the room: a front door with many bolts on it, and two doors that lead to bedrooms.

Even though Artie and his family have lived here eighteen years now, there's still an air of transiency to the room as if they had never unpacked from the time they moved in.

Somebody's at the window, climbing down the fire escape. RONNIE, *Artie's eighteen-year-old son, climbs in the window. He gingerly pulls at the folding gate. It's locked. He stands there for a minute, out of breath.*

*He's a young eighteen. His hair is cropped close
and he wears big glasses. He wears a heavy army
overcoat and under that a suit of army fatigue
clothes.*

*He reaches through the bars to his father's trou-
sers, gets the keys out of the pocket, unlocks the lock,
comes into the room and relocks the gate behind him,
replaces the pants. He tiptoes past his father, who's
still snoring and mumbling:* "Pope Ronnie. Pope
Ronnie. Pope Ronnie."

RONNIE *opens the icebox door, careful not to let
the light spill all over the floor. He takes out milk and
bread.*

The doorbell buzzes.

ARTIE *groans.*

RONNIE *runs into his bedroom.*

*Somebody is knocking on the front door and buzz-
ing quickly, quickly like little mosquito jabs.*

ARTIE *stirs. He unzips himself from his sleeping
bag, runs to the door. He wears ski pajamas. A key
fits into the front door. The door shakes.* ARTIE
*undoes the six bolts that hold the door locked. He
opens the door, dashes back to his bag, and zips himself in.*

BUNNY FLINGUS *throws open the door. The hall
behind her is brilliantly lit. She is a pretty, pink,
slightly plump, electric woman in her late thirties.
She wears a fur-collared coat and plastic booties, and*

two Brownie cameras on cords clunking against a
pair of binoculars.
  At the moment she is freezing, uncomfortable,
and furious.
  She storms to the foot of the couch.

BUNNY: You know what your trouble is? You got no
  sense of history. You know that? Are you aware
  of that? Lock yourself up against history, get
  drowned by the whole tide of human events.
  Sleep it away in your bed. Your bag. Zip yourself
  in, Artie. The greatest tide in the history of the
  world is coming in today, so don't get your feet
  wet.

ARTIE, *picking up his glow-in-the-dark alarm:* It's
  quarter-to-five in the morning, Bunny—

BUNNY: Lucky for you I got a sense of history. *She*
  sits on the edge of the couch; picks up the news-
  paper on the floor. You finished last night's?
  Oooo, it's freezing out there. Breath's coming out
  of everybody's mouth like a balloon in a cartoon.
  She rips the paper into long shreds and stuffs it
  down into the plastic booties she wears.
    People have been up for hours. Queens Bou-
  levard—lined for blocks already! Steam coming
  out of everybody's mouth! Cripples laid out in
  the streets in stretchers with ear muffs on over
  their bandages. Nuns—you never seen so many

nuns in your life! Ordinary people like you and
me in from New Jersey and Connecticut and
there's a lady even drove in from Ohio—Ohio!—
just for today! She drove four of the most crippled people in Toledo. They're stretched out in
the gutter waiting for the sun to come out so
they can start snapping pictures. I haven't seen
so many people, Artie, so excited since the pre-
miere of *Cleopatra*. It's that big. Breathe! There's
miracles in the air!

ARTIE: It's soot, Bunny. Polluted air.

BUNNY: All these out-of-staters driving in with cameras and thermos bottles and you live right here
and you're all zipped in like a turtle. Miss Henshaw, the old lady who's the check-out girl at
A&P who gyps everybody—her nephew is a cop
and she's saving us two divine places right by the
curb. You're not the only one with connections.
But she can't save them forever. Oh God, Artie,
what a morning! You should see the stars!!! I
know all the stars from the time I worked for
that astronomer and you should see Orion—
O'Ryan: the Irish constellation—I haven't looked
up and seen stars in years! I held my autograph
book up and let Jupiter shine on it. Jupiter and
Venus and Mars. They're all out! You got to
come see Orion. He's the hunter and he's pulling
his arrow back so tight in the sky like a Connect-

the-Dots picture made up of all these burning planets. If he ever lets that arrow go, he'll shoot all the other stars out of the sky—what a welcome for the Pope!

And right now, the Pope is flying through that star-filled sky, bumping planets out of the way, and he's asleep dreaming of the mobs waiting for him. When famous people go to sleep at night, it's us they dream of, Artie. The famous ones—they're the real people. We're the creatures of their dreams. You're the dream. I'm the dream. We have to be there for the Pope's dream. Look at the light on the Empire State Building swirling around and around like a burglar's torch looking all through the sky— Everybody's waiting, Artie—everybody!

ARTIE, *angry:* What I want to know is who the hell is paying for this wop's trip over here anyway—

BUNNY, *shocked:* Artie! *Reaches through the bars to close the window.* Ssshhh—they'll hear you—

ARTIE: I don't put my nickels and dimes in Sunday collections to pay for any dago holiday—flying over here with his robes and gee-gaws and bringing his buddies over when I can't even afford a trip to Staten Island—

BUNNY, *puzzled:* What's in Staten Island?

ARTIE: Nothing! But I couldn't even afford a nickel

ferry-boat ride. I known you two months and can't even afford a present for you—a ring—

BUNNY: I don't need a ring—

ARTIE: At least a friendship ring— *He reaches in his sleeping bag and gets out a cigarette and matches and an ashtray.*

BUNNY, *rubbing his head:* I'd only lose it—

ARTIE, *pulling away:* And this guy's flying over here—not tourist—oh no—

BUNNY, *suspicious of his bitterness:* Where'd you go last night?

ARTIE, *back into his bag:* You go see the Pope. Tell him hello for me.

BUNNY: You went to that amateur night, didn't you—

ARTIE, *signaling toward the other room:* Shut up— she's inside—

BUNNY: You went to the El Dorado Bar Amateur Night, didn't you. I spent two months building you up to be something and you throw yourself away on that drivel—

ARTIE: They talked all the way through it—

BUNNY: Did you play them "Where's the Devil in Evelyn?"

ARTIE: They talked and walked around all through it—

BUNNY: I wish I'd been there with you. You know what I would've said to them?

To us: The first time I heard "Mairzy Doats" I realized I am listening to a classic. I picked off "Old Black Magic" and "I Could've Danced All Night" as classics the minute I heard them. *Recites:* "Where is the devil in Evelyn? What's it doing in Angela's eyes?" I didn't work in Macy's Music Department for nix. I know what I'm talking about.

To Artie: That song is a classic. You've written yourself a classic.

ARTIE: I even had to pay for my own beers.

BUNNY: Pearls before swine. Chalk it up to experience.

ARTIE: The blackboard's getting kind of filled up. I'm too old to be a young talent.

BUNNY—*opens the window through the bars:* Smell the bread—

ARTIE: Shut the window—it's freezing and you're letting all the dirt in—

BUNNY: Miss Henshaw's saving us this divine place right by the cemetery so the Pope will have to slow down—

ARTIE: Nothing worse than cold dirt—

The other bedroom door opens and BANANAS SHAUGHNESSY, *a sick woman in a nightgown, looks at them. They don't see her.*

BUNNY, *ecstatically:* And when he passes by in his limousine, I'll call out, "Your Holiness, marry us —the hell with peace to the world—bring peace to us." And he won't hear me because bands will be playing and the whole city yelling, but he'll see me because I been eyed by the best of them, and he'll nod and I'll grab your hand and say, "Marry us, Pope," and he'll wave his holy hand and all the emeralds and rubies on his fingers will send Yes beams. In a way, today's my wedding day. I should have something white at my throat! Our whole life is beginning—my life—our life— and we'll be married and go out to California and Billy will help you. You'll be out there with the big shots—out where you belong—not in any amateur nights in bars on Queens Boulevard. Billy will get your songs in movies. It's not too late to start. With me behind you! Oh, Artie, the El Dorado Bar will stick up a huge neon sign flashing onto Queens Boulevard in a couple of years flashing "Artie Shaughnessy Got Started Here." And nobody'll believe it. Oh, Artie, tables turn.

BANANAS *closes the door.*
ARTIE *gets out of his bag.*

ARTIE, *thoughtfully, sings:*

> Bridges are for burning
> Tables are for turning—

He turns on all the lights. He pulls Bunny by the pudgy arm over to the kitchen.

ARTIE: I'll go see the Pope—

BUNNY, *hugging him:* Oh, I love you!

ARTIE: I'll come if—

BUNNY: You said you'll come. That is tantamount to a promise.

ARTIE: I will if—

BUNNY: Tantamount. Tantamount. You hear that? I didn't work in a law office for nix. I could sue you for breach.

ARTIE, *seductively:* Bunny?

BUNNY, *near tears:* I know what you're going to say—

ARTIE, *opening a ketchup bottle under her nose:* Cook for me?

BUNNY, *in a passionate heat:* I knew it. I knew it.

ARTIE: Just breakfast.

BUNNY: You bend my arm and twist my heart but I got to be strong.

ARTIE: I'm not asking any ten-course dinner.

Bunny runs over to the piano where his clothes are draped to get away from his plea.

BUNNY: Just put your clothes on over the ski p.j.'s I bought you. It's thirty-eight degrees and I don't want you getting your pneumonia back—

ARTIE, *holding up two eggs:* Eggs, baby. Eggs right here.

BUNNY, *holding out his jingling trousers:* Rinse your mouth out to freshen up and come on let's go?

ARTIE, *seductively:* You boil the eggs and pour lemon sauce over—

BUNNY, *shaking the trousers at him:* Hollandaise. I know hollandaise. *Plopping down with the weight of the temptation, glum:* It's really cold out, so dress warm— Look, I stuffed the *New York Post* in my booties—plastic just ain't as warm as it used to be.

ARTIE: And you pour the hollandaise over the eggs on English muffins—and then you put the grilled ham on top— I'm making a scrapbook of all the foods you tell me you know how to cook and then I go through the magazines and cut out pictures of what it must look like. *He gets the scrapbook.* Look—veal parmagina—eggplant meringue.

BUNNY: I cooked that for me last night. It was so good I almost died.

ARTIE—*sings, as Bunny takes the book and looks through it with great despair:*

>If you cooked my words
>Like they was veal
>I'd say I love you
>For every meal.
>Take my words,
>Garlic and oil them,
>Butter and broil them,
>Sauté and boil them—
>Bunny, let me eat you!

Speaks: Cook for me?

BUNNY: Not 'til after we're married.

ARTIE: You couldn't give me a little sample right now?

BUNNY: I'm not that kind of girl. I'll sleep with you anytime you want. Anywhere. In two months I've known you, did I refuse you once? Not once! You want me to climb in the bag with you now? Unzip it—go on—unzip it— Give your fingers a smack and I'm flat on my back. I'll sew those words into a sampler for you in our new home in California. We'll hang it right by the front door. Because, Artie, I'm a rotten lay and I know it and you know it and everybody knows it—

ARTIE: What do you mean? Everybody knows it—

BUNNY: I'm not good in bed. It's no insult. I took

that sex test in the *Reader's Digest* two weeks ago and I scored twelve. Twelve, Artie! I ran out of that dentist office with tears gushing out of my face. But I face up to the truth about myself. So if I cooked for you now and said I won't sleep with you till we're married, you'd look forward to sleeping with me so much that by the time we did get to that motel near Hollywood, I'd be such a disappointment, you'd never forgive me. My cooking is the only thing I got to lure you on with and hold you with. Artie, we got to keep some magic for the honeymoon. It's my first honeymoon and I want it to be so good, I'm aiming for two million calories. I want to cook for you so bad I walk by the A&P, I get all hot jabs of chili powder inside my thighs . . . but I can't till we get those tickets to California safe in my purse, till Billy knows we're coming, till I got that ring right on my cooking finger. . . . Don't tempt me . . . I love you . . .

ARTIE, *beaten:* Two eggs easy over?

BUNNY—*shakes her head No:* And I'm sorry last night went sour . . .

ARTIE—*sits down, depressed:* They made me buy my own beers . . .

BANANAS, *calling from the bedroom:* Is it light? Is it daytime already?

ARTIE *and* BUNNY *look at each other.*

BUNNY: I'll pour you cornflakes.
ARTIE, *nervous:* You better leave.
BUNNY, *standing her ground:* A nice bowlful?
ARTIE: I don't want her to know yet.
BUNNY: It'll be like a coming attraction.
ARTIE, *pushing her into the kitchen:* You're a tease,
    Bunny, and that's the worst thing to be. *He puts
    on his green shirt and pants over his pajamas.*

BANANAS *comes out of the bedroom. She's lived
in her nightgown for the last six months. She's in her
early forties and has been crying for as long as she's
had her nightgown on. She walks uncertainly, as if
hidden barriers lay scattered in her path.*

BANANAS: Is it morning?
ARTIE—*he doesn't know how to cope with her:* Go
    back to bed.
BANANAS: You're dressed and it's so dark. Did you
    get an emergency call? Did the lion have babies
    yet?
ARTIE, *checking that the gate is locked:* The lioness
    hasn't dropped yet. The jaguar and the cheetah
    both still waiting. The birds still on their eggs.
BANANAS: Are you leaving to get away from me?

Tell me? The truth? You hate me. You hate my looks—my face—my clothes—you hate me. You wish I was fatter so there'd be more of me to hate. You hate me. Don't say that! You love me. I know you love me. You love me. Well, I don't love you. How does that grab you? *She is shaking violently.*

ARTIE *takes pills from the piano and holds her and forces the pills in her mouth. He's accepted this as one of the natural facts of his life. There is no violence in the action. Her body shakes. The spasms stop. She's quiet for a long time. He walks over to the kitchen.* BUNNY *kisses the palm of his hand.*

BANANAS: For once could you let my emotions come out? If I laugh, you give me a pill. If I cry, you give me a pill . . . no more pills . . . I'm quiet now . . .

ARTIE *comes out of the kitchen and pours two pills into his hand. He doesn't like to do this.*

BANANAS—*smiles:* No! No more—look at me—I'm a peaceful forest, but I can feel all the animals have gone back into hiding and now I'm very quiet. All the wild animals have gone back into hiding. But once—once let me have an emotion? Let the animals come out? I don't like being still, Artie. It makes me afraid . . .

Brightly: How are you this morning? Sleep well? You were out late last night. I heard you come in and moved over in the bed. Go back to bed and rest. It's still early . . . come back to bed . . .

ARTIE, *finishing dressing:* The Pope is coming today and I'm going to go see him.

BANANAS: The Pope is coming here?

ARTIE: Yes, he's coming here. We're going to kick off our shoes and have a few beers and kick the piano around. *Gently, as if to a child:* The Pope is talking to the UN about Vietnam. He's coming over to stop the war so Ronnie won't have to go to Vietnam.

BANANAS: Three weeks he's been gone. How can twenty-one days be a hundred years?

ARTIE, *to the audience:* This woman doesn't understand. My kid is charmed. He gets greetings to go to .basic training for Vietnam and the Pope does something never done before. He flies out of Italy for the first time *ever* to stop the war. Ronnie'll be home before you can say Jake Rabinowitz. Ronnie—what a kid—a charmed life . . .

BANANAS: I can't go out of the house . . . my fingernails are all different lengths. I couldn't leave the

house. . . . Look—I cut this one just yesterday
and look how long it is already . . . but this one
. . . I cut it months ago right down to the quick
and it hasn't moved that much. I don't understand that. . . . I couldn't see the Pope. I'd embarrass him. My nails are all different. I can feel
them growing . . . they're connected to my veins
and heart and pulling my insides out my fingers.
She is getting hysterical.

ARTIE *forces pills down her mouth. She's quiet.
She smiles at him. Artie's exhausted, upset. He paces
up and down in front of her, loathing her.*

ARTIE: The Pope takes one look at you standing on
Queens Boulevard, he'll make the biggest U-turn
you ever saw right back to Rome. *Angry:* I
dreamed last night Ronnie was the Pope and he
came today and all the streets were lined with
everybody waiting to meet him—and I felt like
Joseph P. Kennedy, only bigger, because the
Pope is a bigger draw than any President. And it
was raining everywhere but on him and when he
saw you and me on Queens Boulevard, he
stopped his glass limo and I stepped into the
bubble, but you didn't. He wouldn't take you.
BANANAS: He would take me!
ARTIE, *triumphant:* Your own son denied you.

Slammed the door in your face and you had open-toe shoes on and the water ran in the heels and out the toes like two Rin Tin Tins taking a leak—and Ronnie and I drove off to the UN and the war in Vietnam stopped and he took me back to Rome and canonized me—made me a Saint of the Church and in charge of writing all the hymns for the Church. A hymn couldn't be played unless it was mine and the whole congregation sang "Where Is the Devil in Evelyn," but they made it sound like monks singing it— You weren't invited, Bananas. Ronnie loved only me. . . . *He finds himself in front of the kitchen. He smiles at Bunny.* What a dream . . . it's awful to have to wake up. For my dreams, I need a passport and shots. I travel the whole world.

BUNNY, *whispering:* I dreamed once I met Abraham Lincoln.

ARTIE: Did you like him?

BUNNY: He was all right. *She opens a jar of pickles and begins eating them.*

BANANAS *sees Bunny's fur coat by Ronnie's room. She opens the front door and throws the coat into the hall. She closes the door behind her.*

BANANAS: You know what I dream? I dream I'm just

waking up and I roam around the house all day crying because of the way my life turned out. And then I do wake up and what do I do? Roam around the house all day crying about the way my life turned out.

ARTIE—*an idea comes to him; he goes to the piano; sings:*

> The day that the Pope came to New York
> The day that the Pope came to New York,
> It really was comical,
> The Pope wore a yarmulke
> The day that the Pope came to New York.

BANANAS: Don't be disrespectful.

She gets up to go to the kitchen. ARTIE *rushes in front of her and blocks her way.* BUNNY *pushes herself against the icebox trying to hide; she's eating a bowl of cornflakes.*

ARTIE: Stay out of the kitchen. I'll get your food—

BANANAS: Chop it up in small pieces . . .

BUNNY, *in a loud, fierce whisper:* Miss Henshaw cannot reserve our places indefinitely. Tantamount to theft is holding a place other people could use. Tantamount. Her nephew the cop could lock us right up. Make her go back to bed.

ARTIE *fixes Bananas' food on a plate.*
BANANAS *sits up on her haunches and puts her hands, palm downwards, under her chin.*

BANANAS: Hello, Artie!
ARTIE: You're going to eat like a human being.
BANANAS: Woof? Woof?
ARTIE: Work all day in a zoo. Come home to a zoo.

He takes a deep breath. He throws her the food. She catches it in her mouth. She rolls on her back.

BANANAS: I like being animals. You know why? I never heard of a famous animal. Oh, a couple of Lassies—an occasional Trigger—but, by and large, animals weren't meant to be famous.

ARTIE *storms into the kitchen.*

BUNNY: What a work of art is a dog. How noble in its thought—how gentle in its dignity—

ARTIE *buries his head against the icebox.*

BANANAS, *smiling out front:* Hello. I haven't had a chance to welcome you. This is my home and I'm your hostess and I should welcome you. I wanted to say Hello and I'm glad you could come. I was very sick a few months ago. I tried to slash my wrists with spoons. But I'm better now and glad to see people. In the house. I couldn't go out. Not yet. Hello. *She walks the length of the stage, smiling at the audience, at us. She has a beautiful smile.*

BUNNY *comes out of the kitchen down to the edge of the stage.*

BUNNY, *to us:* You know what my wish is? The priest told us last Sunday to make a wish when the Pope rides by. When the Pope rides by, the wish in my heart is gonna knock the Pope's eye out. It is braided in tall letters, all *my* veins and arteries and aortas are braided into the wish that she dies pretty soon. *She goes back to the kitchen.*

BANANAS, *who has put a red mask on her head:* I had a vision—a nightmare—I saw you talking to a terrible fat woman with newspapers for feet— and she was talking about hunters up in the sky and that she was a dream and you were a dream . . . *She crosses to the kitchen, puts mask over her eyes and comes up behind Bunny:* Hah!!!

BUNNY *screams in terror and runs into the living room.*

BUNNY: I am not taking insults from a sick person. A healthy person can call me anything they want. But insults from a sickie—a sicksicksickie—I don't like to be degraded. A sick person has fumes in their head—you release poison fumes and it makes me sick—dizzy—like riding the back of a bus. No wonder Negroes are fighting so hard to be freed, riding in the back of busses all those years. I'm amazed they even got enough strength to stand up straight. . . . Where's my coat? Artie, where's my coat? My binox and my camera? *To Bananas:* What did you do with my coat, Looney Tunes?

ARTIE *has retrieved the coat from the hallway.*

You soiled my coat! This coat is soiled! Arthur, are you dressed warm? Are you coming?
ARTIE, *embarrassed:* Bananas, I'd like to present— I'd like you to meet—this is Bunny Flingus.
BUNNY: You got the ski p.j.'s underneath? You used to go around freezing till I met you. I'll teach you how to dress warm. I didn't work at ski lodges for nothing. I worked at Aspen.
BANANAS—*thinks it over a moment:* I'm glad you're making friends, Artie. I'm no good for you.
BUNNY, *taking folders out of her purse, to Bananas:* I might as well give these to you now. Travel fold-

ers to Juarez. It's a simple procedure—you fly down to Mexico—wetback lawyer meets you— sign a paper—jet back to little old N.Y.

ARTIE: Bunny's more than a friend, Bananas.

BUNNY: Play a little music—"South of the Border" —divorce Meheeco style!—

ARTIE: Would you get out of here, Bunny. I'll take care of this.

BANANAS *sings hysterically, without words, "South of the Border."*

BUNNY: I didn't work in a travel agency for nix, Arthur.

ARTIE: Bunny!

BUNNY: I know my way around.

BANANAS *stops singing.*

ARTIE, *taking the folders from Bunny:* She can't even go to the incinerator alone. You're talking about Mexico—

BUNNY: I know these sick wives. I've seen a dozen like you in movies. I wasn't an usher for nothing. You live in wheel chairs just to hold your husband and the minute your husband's out of the room, you're hopped out of your wheel chair doing the Charleston and making a general spectacle of yourself. I see right through you. Tell her, Artie. Tell her what we're going to do.

ARTIE: We're going to California, Bananas.

BUNNY: Bananas! What a name!

BANANAS: A trip would be nice for you . . .

BUNNY: What a banana—

BANANAS: You could see Billy . . . I couldn't see Billy. . . . *Almost laughing:* I can't see anything . . .

ARTIE: Not a trip.

BUNNY: To live. To live forever.

BANANAS: Remember the time we rode up in the elevator with Bob Hope. He's such a wonderful man.

ARTIE: I didn't tell you this, Bunny. Last week, I rode out to Long Island. *To Bananas, taking her hand:* You need help. We—*I* found a nice hosp . . . By the sea . . . by the beautiful sea . . . it's an old estate and you can walk from the train station and it was raining and the roads aren't paved so it's muddy, but by the road where you turn into the estate, there was a tree with blue leaves in the rain— I walked under it to get out of the rain and also because I had never seen a tree with blue leaves and I walked under the tree and all the leaves flew away in one big round bunch—just lifted up, leaving a bare tree. Whoosh. . . . It was birds. Not blue leaves but

Bunny Flingus, Bananas and Artie Shaughnessy

birds, waiting to go to Florida or California . . .
and all the birds flew to another tree a couple of
hundred feet off and that bare tree blossomed—
snap! like that—with all these blue very quiet
leaves. . . . You'll like the place, Bananas. I
talked to the doctor. He had a mustache. You
like mustaches. And the Blue Cross will handle a
lot of it, so we won't have to worry about ex-
pense. . . . You'll like the place . . . a lot of famous people have had crackdowns there, so
you'll be running in good company.

BANANAS: Shock treatments?

ARTIE: No. No shock treatments.

BANANAS: You swear?

BUNNY: If she needs them, she'll get them.

ARTIE: I'm handling this my way.

BUNNY: I'm sick of you kowtowing to her. Those
poison fumes that come out of her head make me
dizzy—suffering—look at her—what does she
know about suffering . . .

BANANAS: Did you read in the paper about the bull
in Madrid who fought so well they didn't let him
die. They healed him, let him rest before they
put him back in the ring, again and again and
again. I don't like the shock treatments, Artie. At
least the concentration camps—I was reading
about them, Artie—they put the people in the
ovens and never took them out—but the shock

treatments—they put you in the oven and then they take you out and then they put you in and then they take you out . . .

BUNNY: Did you read *Modern Screen* two months ago? I am usually not a reader of film magazines, but the cover on it reached right up and seduced my eye in the health club. It was a picture like this—*she clutches her head*—and it was called "Sandra Dee's Night of Hell." Did you read that by any happenstance? Of course you wouldn't read it. You can't see anything. You're ignorant. Not you. Her. The story told of the night before Sandra Dee was to make her first movie and her mother said, "Sandra, do you have everything you need?" And she said—snapped back, real fresh-like—"Leave me alone, Mother. I'm a big girl now and don't need any help from you." So her mother said, "All right, Sandra, but remember I'm always here." Well, her mother closed the door and Sandra could not find her hair curlers anywhere and she was too proud to go to her mom and ask her where they were—

ARTIE: Bunny, I don't understand.

BUNNY: Shut up, I'm not finished yet—and she tore through the house having to look her best for the set tomorrow because it was her first picture and her hair curlers were nowhere! Finally at four in the a.m., her best friend, Annette Funicello, the former Mouseketeer, came over and took the hair curlers out of her very own hair and gave them to Sandra. Thus ended her night of hell, but she had learned a lesson. Suffering—you don't even know the meaning of suffering. You're a nobody and you suffer like a nobody. I'm taking Artie out of this environment and bringing him to California while Billy can still do him some good. Get Artie's songs—his music—into the movies.

ARTIE: I feel I only got about this much life left in me, Bananas. I got to use it. These are my peak years. I got to take this chance. You stay in your room. You're crying. All the time. Ronnie's gone now. This is not a creative atmosphere. . . . Bananas, I'm too old to be a young talent.

BANANAS: I never stopped you all these years . . .

BUNNY: Be proud to admit it, Artie. You were afraid till I came on the scene. Admit it with pride.

ARTIE: I was never afraid. What're you talking about?

BUNNY: No man takes a job feeding animals in the Central Park Zoo unless he's afraid to deal with humans.

ARTIE: I walk right into the cage! What do you mean?

BUNNY: Arthur, I'm trying to talk to your wife. Bananas, I want to be sincere to you and kind.

ARTIE: I'm not afraid of nothing! Put my hand right in the cage—

BUNNY, *sitting down beside Bananas, speaks to her like to a child:* There's a beautiful book of poems by Robert Graves. I never read the book because the title is so beautiful there's no need to read the book: *Man Does. Woman Is.* Look around this apartment. Look at Artie. Look at him.

ARTIE, *muttering:* I been with panthers.

BUNNY, *with great kindness:* I've never met your son, but—no insult to you, Artie—but I don't want to. Man does. What does Artie do? He plays the piano. He creates. What are you? What is Bananas? Like he said before when you said you've been having nightmares. Artie said, "You been looking in the mirror?" Because that's what you are, Bananas. Look in the mirror.

ARTIE *is playing the piano.*

Man Does. Woman Is. I didn't work in a lending library for nothing.

ARTIE: I got panthers licking out of my hands like goddam pussycats.

BUNNY: Then why don't you ever call Billy?

ARTIE: I got family obligations.

BANANAS, *at the window:* You could take these bars down. I'm not going to jump.

BUNNY: You're afraid to call Billy and tell him we're coming out.

BANANAS, *dreamy:* I'd like to jump out right in front of the Pope's car.

ARTIE: Panthers lay right on their backs and I tickle their armpits. You call me afraid? Hah!

BANANAS: He'd take me in his arms and bless me.

BUNNY: Then call Billy now.

ARTIE: It's the middle of the night!

BUNNY: It's only two in the morning out there now.

ARTIE: Two in the morning is the middle of the night!

BUNNY: In Hollywood! Come off it, he's probably not even in yet—they're out there frigging and frugging and swinging and eating and dancing. Since Georgina died, he's probably got a brace of nude starlets splashing in the pool.

ARTIE: I can't call him. He's probably not even in yet—

BUNNY: I don't even think you know him.

ARTIE: Don't know him!

BUNNY: You've been giving me a line—your best friend—big Hollywood big shot—you don't even know him—

ARTIE: Best friends stay your best friends precisely because you don't go calling them in the middle of the night.

BUNNY: You been using him—dangling him over my

head—big Hollywood big-shot friend, just to take advantage of me—just to get in bed with me—casting couches! I heard about them—

ARTIE: That's not true!

BUNNY: And you want me to cook for you! I know the score, baby. I didn't work in a theatrical furniture store for nothing!

She tries to put her coat on to leave. He pulls it off her. If you can't call your best friends in the middle of the night, then who can you call—taking advantage of me in a steam bath—

BANANAS, *picking up the phone:* You want me to get Billy on the phone?

ARTIE: You stay out of this!

BANANAS: He was always my much better friend than yours, Artie.

ARTIE: Your friend! Billy and I only went to kindergarten together, grammar school together, high school together till his family moved away—Fate always kept an eye out to keep us friends. *Sings:*

If you're ever in a jam, here I am.

BANANAS—*sings:*

Friendship.

ARTIE—*sings:*

If you're ever up a tree, just phone me.

He got stationed making training movies and off each reel there's what they call leader—undeveloped film—and he started snipping that leader off, so by the time we all got discharged, he had enough film spliced up to film Twenty Commandments. He made his movie right here on the streets of New York and Rossellini was making his movies in Italy, only Billy was making them here in America and better. He sold everything he had and he made *Conduct of Life* and it's still playing in museums. It's at the Museum of Modern Art next week—and Twentieth Century–Fox signed him and MGM signed him—they both signed him to full contracts—the first time anybody ever got signed by two studios at once. . . . You only knew him about six months' worth, Bananas, when he was making the picture. And everybody in that picture became a star and Billy is still making great pictures.

BUNNY: In his latest one, will you ever forget that moment when Doris Day comes down that flight of stairs in that bathrobe and thinks Rock Hudson is the plumber to fix her bathtub and in reality he's an atomic scientist.

BANANAS: I didn't see that . . .

ARTIE, *mocking:* Bananas doesn't go out of the house . . .

BUNNY, *stars in her eyes:* Call him, Artie.

ARTIE: He gets up early to be on the set. I don't want to wake him up—

BUNNY: Within the next two years, you could be out there in a black tie waiting for the lady—Greer Garson—to open the envelope and say as the world holds its breath—"And the winner of the Oscar for this year's Best Song is—" *She rips a travel folder very slowly.*

ARTIE, *leaning forward:* Who is it? Who won?

BUNNY: And now Miss Mitzi Gaynor and Mr. Franco Corelli of the Metropolitan Opera will sing the winning song for you from the picture of the same name made by his good friend and genius, Billy Einhorn. The winner is of course Mr. Arthur M. Shaughnessy.

ARTIE *goes to the telephone.*

ARTIE—*dials once, then:* Operator, I want to call in Bel Air, Los Angeles—

BUNNY: You got the number?

ARTIE: Tattooed, baby. Tattooed. Your heart and his telephone number right on my chest like a sailor. Not you, operator. I want and fast I want in Los Angeles in Bel Air GR 2-4129 and I will not dial it because I want to speak personally to my good friend and genius, Mr. Billy Einhorn . . . E-I-N—don't you know how to spell it? The name of only Hollywood's leading director my friend and you better not give this number to any

Bunny Flingus and Artie Shaughnessy. *Background:* Bananas
Shaughnessy

of your friends and call him up and bother him
asking for screen tests.

BUNNY: When I was an operator, they made us take
oaths. I had Marlon Brando's number for years
and pistols couldn't've dragged it out of my
head—they make you raise your right hand—

ARTIE: My number is RA 1-2276 and don't go giving
that number away and I want a good connection
. . . hang on, Bunny—*she takes his extended
hand*—you can hear the beepbeepbeeps—we're
traveling across the country—hang on! Ring. It's
ringing. Ring.

BUNNY—*his palm and her palm form one praying
hand:* Oh God, please—

ARTIE, *pulling away from her:* Ring. It's up. Hello?
Billy? Yes, operator, get off—that's Billy. Will
you get off— *To Bunny:* I should've called sta-
tion-to-station. He picked it right up and everything. Billy! This is Ramon Navarro! . . . No,
Billy, it's Artie Shaughnessy. Artie. No, New
York! Did I wake you up! Can you hear me!
Billy, hello! I got to tell you something—first of
all, I got to tell you how bad I feel about Georgina dying—the good die young—what can I
say—and second, since you, you old bum, never
come back to your old stomping grounds—your
happy hunting grounds, I'm thinking of coming
out to see you. . . . I know you can fix up a tour

of the studios and that'd be great . . . and you
can get us hotel reservations—that's just fine.
. . . But, Billy, I'm thinking I got to get away—
not just a vacation—but make a change, get a
break, if you know what I'm getting at. . . . Bananas is fine. She's right here. We were just
thinking about you— No, IT'S NOT FINE. Billy,
this sounds cruel to say but Bananas is as dead
for me as Georgina is for you. I'm in love with a
remarkable wonderful girl—yeah, she's here too
—who I should've married years ago—no, we
didn't know her years ago—I only met her two
months ago—yeah. . . .

*Secretively, pulling the phone off to the cor-
ner:* It's kind of funny, a chimpanzee knocked
me in the back and kinked my back out of whack
and I went to this health club to work it out and
in the steam section with all the steam I got lost
and I went into this steam room and there was
Bunny—yeah, just towels—I mean you could
make a movie out of this, it was so romantic—
She couldn't see me and she started talking about
the weight she had to take off and the food she
had to give up and she started talking about
duckling with orange sauce and oysters baked
with spinach and shrimps baked in the juice of
melted sturgeon eyes which caviar comes from—
well, you know me and food and I got so excited

and the steam's getting thicker and thicker and I
ripped off my towel and kind of raped her . . .
and she was quiet for a long time and then she
finally said one of the greatest lines of all time.
. . . She said, "There's a man in here." . . . And
she was in her sheet like a toga and I was all
toga'd up and I swear, Billy, we were gods and
goddesses and the steam bubbled up and swirled
and it was Mount Olympus. I'm a new man,
Billy—a new man—and I got to make a start before it's too late and I'm calling you, crawling on
my hands and knees—no, not like that, I'm
standing up straight and talking to my best
buddy and saying Can I come see you and bring
Bunny and talk over old times. . . . I'll pay my
own way. I'm not asking you for nothing. Just
your friendship. I think about you so much and I
read about you in the columns and *Conduct of
Life* is playing at the Museum of Modern Art
next week and I get nervous calling you and that
Doris Day pic—well, Bunny and I fell out of our
loge seats—no, Bananas couldn't see it—she
don't go out of the house much. . . . I get nervous about calling you because, well, you know,
and I'm not asking for any Auld Lang Syne treat-
ment, but it must be kind of lonely with Georgina gone and we sent five dollars in to the
Damon Runyon Cancer Fund like Walter Win-

chell said to do and we're gonna send more and it must be kind of lonely and the three of us—Bunny and you and me—could have some laughs. What do you say? You write me and let me know your schedule and we can come any time. But soon. Okay, buddy? Okay? No, this is my call. I'm paying for this call so you don't have to worry—talking to you I get all opened up. You still drinking rye? Jack Daniels! Set out the glasses—open the bottle—no, I'll bring the bottle—we'll see you soon. Good night, Billy. *The call is over.*

Soon, Billy. Soon. Soon. *He hangs up.*

BUNNY, *sings and dances:*

The day that the Pope came to New York
The day that the Pope came to New York,
It really was comical,
The Pope wore a yarmulke
The day that the Pope came to New York!

ARTIE, *stunned:* Did you hear me!

BUNNY: You made me sound like the Moon Coming Over the Mountain! So fat!

ARTIE: He said to say hello to you, Bananas.

BANANAS: Hello . . .

ARTIE, *to Bunny:* Get the copy of *Life* magazine with the story on his house . . .

BUNNY *gets the magazine off the top of the piano.*

BUNNY, *thrilled:* You made me sound so fat! So Kate Smith!

ARTIE, *taking the magazine and opening it:* Look at his house—on the highest part of all Los Angeles—

BUNNY, *devouring the pictures:* It's Bel Air! I know Bel Air! I mean, I don't know Bel Air, but I mean, I know Bel Air!

ARTIE *and* BUNNY *flop on the sofa.* BANANAS, *in the kitchen behind them, throws rice at them.*

BUNNY: Let's get out of here. She gives me the weeping willies.

BANANAS: Oh, no, I'm all right. I was just thinking how lucky we all are. You going off to California and me going off to the loony bin—

ARTIE, *correcting her:* It's a rest place—

BANANAS: With beautiful blue trees, huh?

ARTIE: Birds—waiting to go to Florida or California—

BANANAS: Maybe it was a flock of insane bluebirds that got committed—

ARTIE, *to Bunny:* I'm gonna take a shower. My shirt's all damp from the telephone call.

BUNNY, *putting her coat on:* Artie, I'll be at the corner of Forty-sixth Street near the cemetery by the TV repair store. . . . Hello, John the Baptist. That's who you are. John the Baptist. You called Billy and prepared the way—the way for yourself. Oh, Christ, the dinners I'm gonna cook for you. *Sings:*

> It really was comical,
> The Pope wore a yarmulke
> The day that the Pope came to New York.

She blows a kiss and exits.
ARTIE *yelps triumphantly. He comes downstage.*

ARTIE: Hello, Billy. I'm here. I got all my music. *Sings:*

> I'm here with bells on,
> Ringing out how I feel.
> I'll ring,
> I'll roar,
> I'll sing
> Encore!
> I'm here with bells on.
> Ring! Ring! Ring!

BANANAS, *very depressed:* The people downstairs

. . . they'll be pumping broomsticks on the ceiling . . .

ARTIE, *jubilant:* For once the people downstairs is
Bunny! *Sings:*

For once the people downstairs is Bunny!

He speaks now, jumping up and down on the
floor: Whenever the conversation gets around to
something you don't like, you start ringing bells
of concern for the people downstairs. For once in
my life, the people downstairs is Bunny and I am
a free man! *He bangs all over the keys of the*
piano. And that's a symphony for the people upstairs!

BANANAS: There's just the roof upstairs . . .

ARTIE: Yeah, and you know roofs well. I give up six
months of my life taking care of you and one
morning I wake up and you're gone and all you
got on is a nightgown and your bare feet—the
corns of your bare feet for slippers. And it's
snowing out, snowing a blizzard, and you're out
in it. Twenty-four hours you're gone and the po-
lice are up here and long since gone and you're
being broadcasted for in thirteen states all covered with snow—and I look out that window and
I see a gray smudge in a nightgown standing on
the edge of the roof over there—in a snow bank
and I'm praying to God and I run out of this
place, across the street. And I grab you down

and you're so cold, your nightgown cuts into me like glass breaking and I carried you back here and you didn't even catch a cold—not even a sniffle. If you had just a sniffle, I could've forgiven you. . . . You just look at me with that dead look you got right now. . . . You stay out twenty-four hours in a blizzard hopping from roof to roof without even a pair of drawers on— and *I* get the pneumonia.

BANANAS: Can I have my song?

ARTIE: You're tone-deaf. *Hits two bad notes on the piano.* Like that.

BANANAS: So I won't sing it. . . . My troubles all began a year ago—two years ago today—two days ago today? Today.

ARTIE *plays "The Anniversary Waltz."*

We used to have a beautiful old green Buick. The Green Latrine! . . . I'm not allowed to drive it any more . . . but when I could drive it . . . the last time I drove it, I drove into Manhattan.

ARTIE *plays "In My Merry Oldsmobile."*

And I drive down Broadway—to the Crossroads of the World.

ARTIE *plays "Forty-second Street."*

I see a scene that you wouldn't see in your wild-
est dreams. Forty-second Street. Broadway. Four
corners. Four people. One on each corner. All
waving for taxis. Cardinal Spellman. Jackie Kennedy. Bob Hope. President Johnson. All carrying
suitcases. Taxi! Taxi! I stop in the middle of the
street—the middle of Broadway—and I get out
of my Green Latrine and yell, "Get in. I'm a
gypsy. A gypsy cab. Get in. I'll take you where
you want to go. Don't you all know each other?
Get in! Get in!"
    They keep waving for cabs. I run over to
President Johnson and grab him by the arm.
"Get in!" And pull Jackie Kennedy into my car
and John-John, who I didn't see, starts crying
and Jackie hits me and I hit her and I grab Bob
Hope and push Cardinal Spellman into the back
seat, crying and laughing, "I'll take you where
you want to go. Get in! Give me your suitcases"—
and the suitcases spill open and Jackie Kennedy's
wigs blow down Forty-second Street and Cardinal Spellman hits me and Johnson screams and I
hit him. I hit them all. And then the Green Latrine blew four flat tires and sinks and I run to
protect the car and four cabs appear and all my

friends run into four different cabs. And cars are honking at me to move.

I push the car over the bridge back to Queens. You're asleep. I turn on Johnny Carson to get my mind off and there's Cardinal Spellman and Bob Hope, whose nose is still bleeding, and they tell the story of what happened to them and everybody laughs. Thirty million people watch Johnny Carson and they all laugh. At me. At me. I'm nobody. I knew all those people better than me. You. Ronnie. I know everything about them. Why can't they love me?

And then it began to snow and I went up on the roof . . .

ARTIE, *after a long pause:* Come see the Pope. Pray. Miracles happen. He'll bless you. *Reader's Digest* has an article this month on how prayer answers things. Pray? Kneel down in the street? The Pope can cure you. The *Reader's Digest* don't afford to crap around.

BANANAS: My fingernails are all different lengths. Everybody'd laugh . . .

ARTIE: We used to have fun. Sometimes I miss you so much . . .

BANANAS: *smiling nervously:* If I had gloves to put on my hands . . .

ARTIE: The Pope must be landing now. I'm going to turn on the television. I want you to see him.

Turns on the television. Here he is. He's getting
off the plane. Bananas, look. Look at the screen.
   *He pulls her to the screen. He makes her kneel
in front of it.* Oh God, help Bananas. Please God?
Say a prayer, Bananas. Say, "Make me better,
God . . ."
BANANAS: Make me better, God . . .
ARTIE: "So Artie can go away in peace." . . . Here's
the Pope. *He speaks to the screen.* Get out of the
way! Let a sick woman see! There he is! Kiss
him? Kiss his hem, Bananas. He'll cure you! Kiss
him.

BANANAS *leans forward to kiss the screen. She
looks up and laughs at her husband.*

BANANAS: The screen is so cold . . .
ARTIE, *leaping:* Get out of the way, you goddam
newsman! *He pushes Bananas aside and kisses
the screen.* Help me—help me—Your Holiness . . .

*While he hugs the set, Bananas leaves the room
to go into her bedroom.*
   The front door flies open. BUNNY *bursts in,
flushed, bubbling. She has an enormous "I Love
Paul" button on her coat.*

BUNNY: He's landed! He's landed! It's on every-body's transistors and you're still here! And the school kids!—the Pope drives by, he sees all those school kids, he's gonna come out for birth control today!! Churches will be selling Holy Di-aphragms with pictures of Saint Christopher and saints on them. You mark my words.

To us, indicating her button: They ran out of "Welcome Pope" buttons so I ran downstairs and got my leftover from when the Beatles were here! I am famished! What a day! *She goes to the icebox and downs a bottle of soda.*

BANANAS *comes out of the bedroom. A coat over her nightgown. A hat cocked on her head. Two dif-ferent shoes, one higher than the other. She is smil-ing. She is pulling on gloves.*

ARTIE *turns off the TV.*

BUNNY *gapes. Band music plays joyously in the distance.*

ARTIE *goes to Bananas and takes her arm.*

BUNNY: Now wait one minute. Miss Henshaw is going to be mighty pissed off.

ARTIE: Just for today.

BANANAS: Hold me tight . . .

ARTIE, *grabbing his coat:* Over the threshold . . .

They go out.

BUNNY: Artie, are you dressed warm? Are you dressed warm? Your music! You forgot your music! You gotta get it blessed by the Pope!!

BANANAS *appears in the doorway and grabs the music from Bunny.*

BANANAS—*sings:*

It really was comical,
The Pope wore a yarmulke
The day that the Pope came to New York.

BUNNY: You witch! You'll be in Bellevue tonight with enough shock treatments they can plug Times Square into your ear. I didn't work for Con Edison for nothing! *She storms out after them. Slams the door behind her.*

The bedroom door RONNIE *went into at the beginning of the act opens. He comes out carrying a large gift box.*
He comes downstage and stares at us.

CURTAIN

Act

Two

SCENE 1

RONNIE *is standing in the same position, staring at us. He takes two hand grenades out of the pockets of his fatigues, wire, his father's alarm clock. He wires them together, setting the alarm on the clock at a special time. He puts the whole device into the gift box.*

He is very young—looks barely seventeen—his hair is cropped close all over; he is tall, skinny. He speaks with deep, suffocated, religious fervor; his

*eyes bulge with a strange mixture of terrifying inno-
cence and diabolism. You can't figure out whether
he'd be a gargoyle on some Gothic cathedral or a
skinny cherub on some altar.*

RONNIE: My father tell you all about me? Pope Ronnie? Charmed life? How great I am? That's how
he is with you. You should hear him with me,
you'd sing a different tune pretty quick, and it
wouldn't be "Where Is the Devil in Evelyn?"

*He goes into his room and returns carrying a
large, dusty box. He opens it and takes out an altar
boy's bright red cassock and white surplice that used
to fit him when he was twelve. As he puts them on,
he speaks to us:*

I was twelve years old and all the newspapers
had headlines on my twelfth birthday that Billy
was coming to town. And *Life* was doing stories
on him and *Look* and the newsreels, because
Billy was searching America to find the Ideal
American Boy to play Huckleberry Finn. And
Billy came to New York and called my father and
asked him if he could stay here—Billy needed a
hide-out. In Waldorf Astorias all over the country, chambermaids would wheel silver carts to
change the sheets. And out of the sheets would

hop little boys saying, "Hello, I'm Huckleberry Finn." All over the country, little boys dressed in blue jeans and straw hats would be sent to him in crates, be under the silver cover covering his dinner, in his medicine cabinet in all his hotel rooms, his suitcase—"Hello, Hello, I'm Huckleberry Finn." And he was coming here to hide out. Here—Billy coming here— I asked the nun in school who was Huckleberry Finn—

The nun in Queen of Martyrs knew. She told me. The Ideal American Boy. And coming home, all the store windows reflected me and the mirror in the tailor shop said, "Hello, Huck." The butcher shop window said, "Hello, Huck. Hello, Huckleberry Finn. All America Wants to Meet Billy and He'll Be Hiding Out in Your House." I came home—went in there—into my room and packed my bag. . . . I knew Billy would see me and take me back to California with him that very day. This room smelled of ammonia and air freshener and these slipcovers were new that day and my parents were filling up the icebox in their brand-new clothes, filling up the icebox with food and liquor as excited as if the Pope was coming—and nervous because they hadn't seen him in a long while—Billy. They told me my new clothes were on my bed. To go get dressed. I didn't want to tell them I'd be leaving shortly to start a new life. That I'd be flying out to California with Billy on the H.M.S. Huckleberry. I didn't want tears from them—only trails of envy. . . . I went to my room and packed my bag and waited.

The doorbell rang. *He starts hitting two notes on the piano.* If you listen close, you can still hear the echoes of those wet kisses and handshakes and tears and backs getting hit and Hello, Billys, Hello. They talked for a long time about people from their past. And then my father called out, "Ronnie, guess who? Billy, we named him after your father. Ronnie, guess who?"

I picked up my bag and said good-bye to myself in the mirror. Came out. Billy there. Smiling.

It suddenly dawned on me. You had to do things to get parts.

I began dancing. And singing. Immediately. Things I have never done in my life—before or since. I stood on my head and skipped and whirled—*He cartwheels across the stage*—spectacular leaps in the air so I could see veins in the ceiling—ran up and down the keys of the piano and sang and began laughing and crying soft and loud to show off all my emotions. And I heard music and drums that I couldn't even keep up with. And then cut off all my emotions just like that. Instantly. And took a deep bow like the

Dying Swan I saw on Ed Sullivan. I picked up my suitcase and waited by the door.

Billy turned to my parents, whose jaws were down to about there, and Billy said, "You never told me you had a mentally retarded child."

"You never told me I had an idiot for a godchild," and I picked up my bag and went into my room and shut the door and never came out the whole time he was here.

My only triumph was he could never find a Huckleberry Finn. Another company made the picture a few years later, but it flopped.

My father thinks I'm nothing. Billy. My sergeant. They laugh at me. You laughing at me? I'm going to fool you all. By tonight, I'll be on headlines all over the world. Cover of *Time. Life.* TV specials. *He shows a picture of himself on the wall.* I hope they use this picture of me—I look better with hair— Go ahead—laugh. Because you know what I think of you? *He gives us hesitant Bronx cheers.* I'm sorry you had to hear that —pay seven or eight dollars to hear that. But I don't care. I'll show you all. I'll be too big for any of you.

The sound of a key in the door. ARTIE *is heard singing* "The Day That the Pope Came to New York."

RONNIE *exits to his room, carrying the gift box containing the bomb.*

ARTIE: Bunny says, "Arthur, I am not talking to you but I'll say it to the breeze: Arthur, get your music. 'Bring On the Girls.' Hold up your music for when the Pope His Holiness rides by." *To us:* You heard these songs. They don't need blessings. I hate to get all kissyass, you know? But it can't hurt. "Bring On the Girls." Where is it? Whenever Bunny cleans up in here you never can find anything. You should see the two girls holding each other up like two sisters and they're not even speaking which makes them even more like sisters. Wouldn't it be great if they fell in love and we all could stay . . .

A beautiful girl in a fur coat stands hesitantly in the doorway. She carries flowers and liquor in her arms. She is CORRINNA STROLLER.

CORRINNA: Mr. Shaughnessy?
ARTIE: Did I win something? Where'd I put those sweepstake tickets—I'll get them—
CORRINNA: Oh oh oh ohhhhh—it's just like Billy said. Oh God, it's like walking into a photo album. Norman Rockwell. Grandma Moses. Let me look at you. Oh, I was afraid with the Pope,

you'd be out, but it's just like Billy said. You're
here!

ARTIE: Billy? We talked this morning . . .

CORRINNA: Billy called me just as I was checking
out and told me to stop by on my way to the airport.

ARTIE: A friend of Billy's and you stay in a hotel?
Don't you know any friend of Billy's has a per-
manent address right here. . . . Don't tell
me . . .

CORRINNA: What?

ARTIE: I know your name.

CORRINNA, *very pleased:* Oh, how could you . . .

ARTIE: You're Corrinna Stroller.

CORRINNA, *modestly:* Oh . . .

ARTIE: I knew it. I saw that one movie you made for
Billy . . .

CORRINNA: That's how we met.

ARTIE: And then you retired—

CORRINNA—*a sore point:* Well . . .

ARTIE: You were fantastic.

CORRINNA: Well . . .

ARTIE: Why did you quit?

CORRINNA: Well . . .

ARTIE: Will you sit down for a few minutes? Just let
me get my girls. If you left without seeing them.
. . . *He comes down to us.* You call Billy and he
sends stars. Stars! *To Corrinna:* The icebox is

yours. I'll be right back. Corrinna Stroller! *He exits.*

CORRINNA *is alone. There is a high, loud whine. Her hands go to her ears. The whine becomes very electronic. The sound is almost painful. She pulls a hearing aid from each ear. The sound suddenly stops. She reaches into her dress and removes a receiver that the aids are wired to.*
She crosses to the couch and sits.

CORRINNA, *to us:* Don't tell—please? I don't want them to know I'm deaf. I don't want them to think Billy's going around with some deaf girl. There was an accident on a set—a set of Billy's. . . . I can hear with my transistors. *She shows them to us.* I want them to know me first. So please, don't tell. Please.

BUNNY *enters with* ARTIE *close behind.*

BUNNY: Where is she? Where is she? Oh . . . Corrinna Stroller! Limos in the streets. Oh, Miss Stroller, I only saw your one movie, *Warmonger,* but it is permanently enshrined in the Loew's of my heart. *To us:* That scene where she blows up in the landmine—so realistic. *To Corrinna:* And

Corrinna Stroller

then you never made another picture. What happened?

CORRINNA: I just dropped in to say hi—

BUNNY: Hi! Oh, Corrinna Stroller! *To Artie:* You know that phony Mrs. Binard in 4-C who wouldn't give you the time of day—she says, "Oh Miss Flingus, is this limo connected to you?" I'd like to put my fist through her dimple. *She takes the newspapers out of her booties. To Corrinna:* Hi, I'm Bunny, the future His. You want some snacks?

CORRINNA: I've got to catch a plane—

BUNNY: Should I send some down to the chauffeur? Oh, stay, have some snacks—

ARTIE: Are you gonna cook?

BUNNY: Just short-order snacks, while you audition . . .

ARTIE: Audition?

BUNNY: You get your ass on those tunes while the Pope's blessing is still hot on them. Artie, the Pope looked right at me! We're in solid. *To Corrinna, with a tray of celery:* Ta Ta!! That's a trumpet. Look, before we start chattering about hellos and how-are-yous and who we all are and old times and new times, bite into a celery for some quick energy and I'll get you a soda and Arthur here writes songs that could be perfect for Oscar-winning medleys and love themes of important motion-picture presentations and you should tell Billy about it. Artie being the Webster's Dictionary Definition for Mr. Shy. *Gone with the Wind. The Wizard of Oz.* That is the calibre of film that I am talking about. And His Holiness the Very Same Pope has seen these songs and given them his blessings. *She shows the sheet music to Corrinna.*

CORRINNA: I'd love to, but I have a very slight postnasal drip.

BUNNY: Isn't she wonderful! Go on, Artie, while Mister Magic still shimmers!

ARTIE, *at the piano, sings:*

> Back together again,
> Back together again.
> *etc.*

THREE NUNS *appear at the window.*

CORRINNA *sees them and screams. Her transistors fall on the floor.*

CORRINNA: My transistors!! *She is down on her knees, searching for them.*

BUNNY: Get away from here! Scat! Get away! Go! Go!

HEAD NUN: We got locked out on your roof! Please,

it's fifty below and our fingers are icicles and our lips are the color of Mary—

SECOND NUN: The doorknob came right off in our hands—

ARTIE: I'm sorry, Sisters, but these are secret auditions . . .

HEAD NUN: But we missed the Pope! And we came all the way from Ridgewood! Let us see it on television!

ALL THREE NUNS: Please! Please! On television!

ARTIE, *opening the gate:* Oh, all right . . .

BUNNY: Don't do it, Arthur. *She sees Corrinna on the floor.* What's the matter, honey, did you drop something? It's like a regular Vatican here.

During the scene CORRINNA *will pick up her transistors at any moment she feels she is not being observed. She keeps them in a small vial for safety.*

SECOND NUN—*they are inside now:* We stole Monsignor Boyle's binoculars!

HEAD NUN: We couldn't see the Pope, the crowds were so thick, so we climbed up onto your roof . . .

SECOND NUN: And I put the binoculars up to my eyes and got the Pope in focus and the pressure of Him against my eyes, oh God, the binoculars

flew out of my hands like a miracle in re-
verse . . .

HEAD NUN: We'll be quiet.

LITTLE NUN, *in the kitchen:* Look! Peanut butter!
They have peanut butter! *To us:* We're not allowed peanut butter!

ARTIE: Put that away!

HEAD NUN, *a sergeant:* You! Get over here.

The LITTLE NUN *obeys.* ARTIE *turns on the TV.*

SECOND NUN: Oh, color. They don't have color!

HEAD NUN: Would you have some beers? To warm
us up? We will pray for you many years for your
kindness today.

BANANAS, *offstage, in the hall, terrified:* Artie? Artie,
are you there? Is this my home? Artie?

ARTIE: Oh God, Bananas. Bunny, get the beers,
would you?

BUNNY: What do I look like?

ARTIE *runs into the hall to retrieve Bananas.*

BUNNY, *to Corrinna:* Excuse the interruption; we're
not religious as such, but his heart is the Sistine
Chapel. *She goes to the kitchen for beers.*

BANANAS, *entering with Artie:* I didn't know where

home was. Miss Henshaw showed me. And then your fat girlfriend ran away. I had to ask directions how to get back.

BUNNY *plunks the beers on the TV set.*

SECOND NUN: Oh, imported! They don't have imported! We could've stayed back in Ridgewood and watched color and had imported, but no, she's got to see everything in the flesh—

HEAD NUN: You were the one who dropped the binoculars—

SECOND NUN: You were the one who stole them—

BANANAS: Artie, did you bring work home from the office?

ARTIE: They're nuns, Bananas, nuns.

HEAD NUN: We got locked out on the upstairs roof. Hi!

BANANAS: Hi!

ARTIE: This is Corrinna Stroller, Billy's girlfriend. Corrinna, this is Bananas.

THE NUNS: Corinna Stroller! The movie star!

BANANAS: Hello, Billy's girlfriend. God, Billy's girlfriends always make me feel so shabby!

BUNNY, *to Corrinna:* Arthur believes in keeping family skeletons out in the open like pets. Heel, Bananas, heel!

LITTLE NUN, *running to Corrinna's side, to Corrinna:* I saw *The Sound of Music* thirty-one times. It changed my entire life.
CORRINNA: Unitarian.
ARTIE: All right now, where were we?
BUNNY: Ta Ta! The trumpet.
ARTIE, *at the piano, sings:*

> Back together again,
> Back together again . . .

HEAD NUN—*screams:* There's Jackie Kennedy!!! Get me with Jackie Kennedy!!! *She puts her arm around the TV.*

The LITTLE NUN *takes out her Brownie with flash and takes a picture of the head nun posing with Jackie on TV.*

SECOND NUN: There's Mayor Lindsay! Get me with him! Mayor Lindsay dreamboat! Mayor Wagner ugh!

There is a scream from the kitchen. BANANAS *has burned herself.*

ARTIE, *running into kitchen:* What do you think you're doing?

BANANAS: Cooking for our guests. I'm some good, Artie. I can cook.

ARTIE: What is it?

BANANAS: Hamburgers. I felt for them and I cooked them.

ARTIE: Brillo pads. You want to feed our guests Brillo pads? *To the nuns:* Sisters, please, you're going to have to go into the other room. You're upsetting my wife. *He unplugs the TV and hustles the nuns off into Ronnie's bedroom.*

SECOND NUN: Go on with what you're doing. Don't bother about us. We're nothing. We've just given our lives up praying for you. I'm going to start picking who I pray for. *She exits.*

The LITTLE NUN *crosses to the kitchen to retrieve the peanut butter.*

BUNNY: That man is a saint. That woman is a devil.

BANANAS: I'm burned.

BUNNY: Put some vinegar on it. Some salt. Take the sting out.

HEAD NUN, *coming out of the bedroom, very pleased:* There is an altar boy in here. *She exits.*

BANANAS: My son was an altar boy. He kept us in good with God. But then he grew up. He isn't an altar boy any more. *She exits into her room.*

BUNNY, *to Corrinna:* Sometimes I think the whole world has gone cuckoo, don't you?
CORRINNA: For two days.

The LITTLE NUN *goes into Ronnie's room as* ARTIE *comes out and downstage.*

ARTIE, *to us:* My son Ronnie's in there! He's been picked to be the Pope's altar boy at Yankee Stadium—out of all the boys at Fort Dix! I tell you —miracles tumble down on this family. I don't want you to meet him yet. If his mother sees him, her head will go all over the wall like Spanish omelettes. *To Corrinna:* Are you comfortable?
BUNNY: She's adorable! And so down to earth! *She takes Corrinna's bejeweled hands.*
CORRINNA: It's five carats. It's something, isn't it?
BUNNY, *to Corrinna:* Sit right up here with Mister Maestro— *She seats Corrinna next to Artie at the piano.*
ARTIE: Where was I—
BUNNY: "Like Fido chewed them." You left off there—
ARTIE—*sings as* BUNNY *dances.* BANANAS *enters and watches them.*

> . . . Like Fido chewed them,
> But we're

Back together again.
You can say you knew us when
We were together;
Now we're apart,
Thunder and lightning's
Back in my heart,
And that's the weather to be
When you're back together with me.

BUNNY *claps wildly.* CORRINNA *follows suit.* BA-
NANAS *claps slowly.*

BUNNY: Encore! Encore!

ARTIE, *happy now:* What should I play next?

BUNNY: Oh God, how do you pick a branch from a
whole Redwood Forest?

BANANAS, *licking her hand:* "I Love You So I Keep
Dreaming."

BUNNY—*picks up the phone, but doesn't dial:* Come
and get her!

BANANAS: Play "I Love You So I Keep Dreaming."

ARTIE, *pleased:* You really remember that?

BANANAS: How could I forget it . . .

BUNNY: I'm not used to being Queen of the Outsid-
ers. What song is this?

ARTIE: I almost forgot it. It must have been like
Number One that I ever wrote. The one that
showed me I should go on.

BUNNY: Well, let me hear it.

ARTIE: You really surprise me, Bananas. Sometimes I miss you so much . . .

BUNNY—*a warning:* Arthur, I still haven't forgiven you for this morning.

ARTIE—*sings:*

> I love you so I keep dreaming
> Of all the lovely times we shared . . .

BUNNY: Heaven. That is unadulterated heaven.

BANANAS, *interrupting:* Now play "White Christmas"?

BUNNY: Shocks for sure.

BANANAS, *banging the keys of the piano:* Play "White Christmas"?

ARTIE, *to Corrinna:* She's . . . not feeling too . . . hot . . .

BUNNY, *to Corrinna:* In case you haven't noticed . . .

ARTIE: She keeps crawling under the weather. . . . *He plays a run on the piano.*

BANANAS: "White Christmas"???????

ARTIE *groans; plays and sings "White Christmas."*

BUNNY, *to Corrinna:* It really burns me up all these years The Telephone Hour doing salutes to fak-

ers like Richard Rodgers. Just listen to that.
Blaaaagh.

ARTIE *stops playing.*

BANANAS: Don't you hear it?
ARTIE—*plays and sings slowly:*
> I'm dreaming of a . . .
> I love you so I . . .

They are the same tune. Oh God. Oh God.
BANANAS—*sings desperately:*
> I love you so I keep dreaming—

Are you tone deaf? Can't you hear it? *She bangs
the keys on the piano.*

ARTIE *slams the lid shut on her hand. She yells
and licks her fingers to get the pain off them.*

ARTIE: Oh, you have had it, Little Missy. All these
years you knew that and made me play it. She's
always trying to do that, Corrinna. Always trying
to embarrass me. You have had it, Little Missy.
Did Shakespeare ever write one original plot?
You tell me that?
> *He drags Bananas down to the edge of the*

stage. To us: In front of all of you, I am sorry. But you are looking at someone who has had it.

BANANAS: I am just saying your song sounds an awful lot like "White—

ARTIE: Then they can sing my song in the summertime. *He pushes her away, and picks up the phone.*

BANANAS: Who are you calling?

BUNNY: Do it, Arthur.

BANANAS, *terrified:* Artie, who are you calling??????

BUNNY: Do you have a little suitcase? I'll start you packing.

BANANAS, *to Corrinna:* Billy's friend? Help me? Billy wouldn't want them to do this. Not to me. He'd be mad. *Whispering desperately, grabbing Corrinna's hands:* Help me? Bluebirds. He'll tell you all about it. Me walking on the roof. Can't you say anything? You want bribes? Here—take these flowers. They're for you. Take this liquor. For you. *She is hysterical.*

BUNNY *pulls her away and slaps her.*

I'll be quiet. I'll take my pills. *She reaches for the vial containing Corrinna's transistors and swallows them.*

CORRINNA, *to us:* My transistors!

ARTIE, *on the telephone:* This is Mr. Shaughnessy.

Arthur M. . . . I was out there last week and
talked about my wife.

BANANAS: That's why my ears were burning . . .

ARTIE: I forgot which doctor I talked to.

BANANAS: He had a mustache.

ARTIE: He had a mustache. *To his wife:* Thank you.
Into phone: Doctor? Hello? That's right, Doctor,
could you come and . . . all that we talked
about. The room over the garage is fine. Yes,
Doctor. Now. Today. . . . Really? That soon?
She'll be all ready. . . . *He hangs up the phone.*

BUNNY: Arthur, give me your hand. Like I said, today's my wedding day. I wanted something
white at my throat. Look, downstairs in a pink
cookie jar, I got a thousand dollars saved up and
we are flying out to California with Corrinna. As
soon as Bananas here is carted off, we'll step off
that plane and Billy and you and I and Corrinna
here will eat and dance and drink and love until
the middle of the next full moon. *To Bananas:*
Bananas, honey, it's not just a hospital. They got
dances. *To Corrinna:* Corrinna, I'll be right back
with my suitcase. *To Artie:* Artie, start packing.
All my life I been treated like an old shoe. You
turned me into a glass slipper. *Sings:*

I'm here with bells on.
Ring! Ring! Ring! Ring! Ring!

She exits.

ARTIE: I'm sorry. I'm sorry.

BANANAS *runs into her bedroom.*
CORRINNA *edges toward the front door.*

Well, Corrinna, now you know everything. Dirty laundry out in the open. I'll be different out West. I'm great at a party. I never took a plane trip before. I guess that's why my stomach is all queazied up. . . . Hey, I'd better start packing. . . . *He exits.*

CORRINNA *heads for the door. The* NUNS *enter.*

HEAD NUN: Miss Stroller! Miss Stroller! He told us all about Hollywood and Billy and Huckleberry Finn—

SECOND NUN: You tell Billy he ought to be ashamed treating a boy like that—

LITTLE NUN, *with paper and pen:* Miss Stroller, may I have your autograph?

CORRINNA: Sisters, pray for me? Pray my ears come out all right. I'm leaving for Australia—

THE NUNS: Australia?!?

CORRINNA: For a very major ear operation and I need all the prayers I can get. *To us:* South Africa's where they do the heart work, but Australia's the place for ears. So pray for me. Pray my operation's a success.

ARTIE *enters with his suitcase half-packed.*

ARTIE: Australia?

CORRINNA: I'm so glad I made a new friend my last
day in America.

THE NUNS: She's going to Australia!

CORRINNA: Perhaps you'll bring me luck.

ARTIE: Your last day in America? Sisters, please.

CORRINNA: I'll be Mrs. Einhorn the next time you
see me. . . . Billy and I are off to Australia tomorrow for two fabulous years. Billy's making a
new film that is an absolute breakthrough for
him—*Kangaroo*—and you must—all of you—
come to California.

THE NUNS: *Kangaroo!* California!

CORRINNA: And we'll be back in two years.

ARTIE: But we're coming with you today . . .

The NUNS *are praying for Corrinna.*

LITTLE NUN: Our Father, who art in heaven . . .

SECOND NUN: You shut up. I want to pray for her.
Our Father—

HEAD NUN—*blows whistle:* I'll pray for her. *Sings:*

Ave Maria—

The THREE NUNS *sing "Ave Maria."*

RONNIE *enters wearing his army overcoat over*

the altar boy's cassock and carrying the box with the bomb. He speaks over the singing.

RONNIE: Pop! Pop! I'm going!

ARTIE: Ronnie! Corrinna, this is the boy. *To us:* He's been down at Fort Dix studying to be a general—

RONNIE: Pop, I'm going to blow up the Pope.

ARTIE: See how nice you look with your hair all cut—

The NUNS *have finished singing "Ave Maria" and take flash pictures of themselves posing with Corrinna.*

RONNIE: Pop, I'm going to blow up the Pope and when *Time* interviews me tonight, I won't even mention you. I'll say I was an orphan.

ARTIE: Ronnie, why didn't you write and let me know you were coming home. I might've been in California—it's great to see you—

CORRINNA *runs up to the front door, then stops.*

CORRINNA: Oh, wait a minute. The Pope's Mass at Yankee Stadium! I have two tickets for the Pope's Mass at Yankee Stadium. Would anybody like them?

The NUNS *and* RONNIE *rush Corrinna for the tickets, forcing her back against the door.* RONNIE *wins
the tickets and comes downstage to retrieve his gift-
wrapped bomb. When he turns around to leave, the*
THREE NUNS *are advancing threateningly on him.
They will not let him pass. They lunge at him. He
runs into the bedroom for protection.*

ARTIE, *at the front door:* Miss Stroller, two years?
Let's get this Australia part straight. Two years?

An M.P. *steps between Artie and Corrinna and
marches into the room. The* M.P. *searches the room.*
Who are you? What are you doing here? Can
I help you?
CORRINNA: Oh! This must be Ronnie! The son in the
Army! I can't *wait* to hear all about you! *She em-
braces the M.P.*

The M.P. *hears the noises and fighting from
Ronnie's room and runs in there.*

CORRINNA, *to Artie:* He looks just like you!
ARTIE, *following the M.P.:* You can't barge into a
house like this—where are you going?

The LITTLE NUN *runs out of the bedroom, triumphantly waving the tickets, almost knocking Artie
over.*

LITTLE NUN: I got 'em! I got 'em!

RONNIE *runs out after her. The other* TWO NUNS *run after him. The* M.P. *runs after them.* RONNIE *runs into the kitchen after the* LITTLE NUN, *who leaps over the couch.* RONNIE *leaps after her. He lands on top of her. He grabs the tickets.*

HEAD NUN, *to the M.P.:* Make him give us back our tickets.

M.P.—*a deep breath and then:* Ronald-V.-Shaugh-nessy.-You-are-under-arrest-for-being-absent-without-leave.-You-have-the-right-to-remain-si-lent.-I-must-warn-you-that-anything-you-say-may-be-used-against-you-in-a-military-court-of-law.-You-have-the-right-to-counsel.-Do-you-wish-to-call-counsel?

RONNIE *attempts escape. The* HEAD NUN *grabs him.*

HEAD NUN: That altar boy stole our tickets!
SECOND NUN: Make him give them back to us!

RONNIE *throws the tickets down. The* HEAD NUN *grabs them.*

HEAD NUN, *to the little nun:* You! Back to Ridgewood! Yahoo! *She exits.*

SECOND NUN, *to Corrinna:* Good luck with your ear
operation. *She exits.*

CORRINNA: This is an invitation—come to California.

RONNIE, *tossing the bomb to Corrinna:* From me to
Billy—

CORRINNA: Oh, how sweet. I can't wait to open it.
Hold the elevator!! *She runs out.*

ARTIE, *to the M.P., who is struggling with Ronnie:*
Hey, what are you doing to my boy?!?

A MAN dressed in medical whites enters.

WHITE MAN: I got a radio message to pick up a Mrs.
Arthur M. Shaughnessy.

ARTIE: Bananas! *He runs to her bedroom.*

BUNNY, *dancing in through the front door, beaming
and dressed like a million bucks:* Ta Ta! An-
nouncing Mrs. Arthur M. Shaughnessy!

WHITE MAN: That's the name. Come along.

BUNNY, *to us, sings:*

> I'm here with bells on,
> Ringing out how I feel . . .

*The WHITE MAN slips the strait jacket on Bunny.
She struggles. He drags her out. She's fighting wildly.*

ARTIE: Wait. Stop.

RONNIE *pulls him from the door as there is a terrible explosion. Pictures fly off the wall. Smoke pours in from the hall.*

BUNNY, *entering through the smoke:* Artie? Where's Corrinna? Where's Corrinna?
ARTIE: Corrinna?

ARTIE *runs out into the hall with* BUNNY.
The lights dim as RONNIE *and the* M.P. *grapple in slow motion, the* LITTLE NUN *trying to pull the M.P. off Ronnie.*
BANANAS *comes downstage into the light. An unattached vacuum hose is wrapped around her shoulders. She cleans the floor with the metallic end of the hose. She smiles at us.*

BANANAS, *to us:* My house is a mess. . . . Let me straighten up. . . . I can do that. . . . I'm a housewife. . . . I'm good for something. . . . *Sings as she vacuums:*

I love you so I keep dream . . .

Closes her eyes. Artie, you could salvage that song. You really could.

CURTAIN

SCENE 2

In the darkness after the curtain we hear the POPE *from Yankee Stadium.*

VOICE OF THE POPE: We feel, too, that the entire American people is here present with its noblest and most characteristic traits: a people basing its conception of life on spiritual values, on a religious sense, on freedom, on loyalty, on work, on the respect of duty, on family affection, on generosity and courage—

The curtain goes up.
It is later that night and the only illumination in the room is the light from the television.
The house is vaguely picked up but not repaired, and everything is askew; neat—things are picked up off the floor for instance—but lampshades are just tilted enough, pictures on the wall just slanted enough, and we see that everything that had been on the floor—the clothes, the suitcases—has been jammed into corners.
ARTIE *is watching the television.*
Another person is sitting in the easy chair in front of the TV.

—safeguarding the American spirit from those dangers which prosperity itself can entail and which the materialism of our day can make even more menacing. . . . From its brief but heroic history, this young and flourishing country can derive lofty and convincing examples to encourage it all in its future progress.

From the easy chair, we hear sobbing. The deep sobbing of a man.
ARTIE *clicks off the television and clicks on the lights. He has put a coat and tie over his green park clothes. He's very uncomfortable and is trying to be very cheery. The* MAN *in the chair keeps sobbing.*

ARTIE: I'm glad he said that. That Pope up at Yankee Stadium—some guy. Boy, isn't that Pope some guy. You ever met him in your travels? . . . You watch. That gang war in Vietnam—over tomorrow . . .
Brightly: People always talking about a certain part of the anatomy of a turkey like every Thanksgiving you say give me the Pope's nose. But that Pope is a handsome guy. Not as good-looking as you and me, but clean. Businesslike.
To us: This is the one. The only. You guessed it: this is Billy. He got here just before the eleven o'clock news. He had to identify Corrinna's body, so he's a little upset. You forgive him, okay?

Billy, come on—don't take it so hard. . . .
You want to take off your shoes? . . . You want
to get comfortable? . . . You want a beer? . . .
He sits at the piano; plays and sings:

> If there's a broken heart
> For every light on Broadway,
> Screw in another bulb . . .

You like that? . . . Look, Billy, I'm sorry as hell
we had to get together this way. . . . Look at it
this way. It was quick. No pain. Pain is awful but
she was one of the luckies, Bill. She just went.
And the apartment is all insured. They'll give us
a new elevator and everything.

BILLY: The one thing she wanted was . . .

ARTIE: Come on, boy. Together. Cry, cry, get it all
out.

BILLY: She wanted her footprints in Grauman's Chinese. I'm going to have her shoes set in wet ce-
ment. A ceremony. A tribute. God knows she'd
hate it.

ARTIE: Hate it?

BILLY: Ahh, ever since the ears went, she stopped
having the push, like she couldn't hear her different drummer any more, drumming up all that
push to get her to the top. She just stopped. *He
cries. Deep sobs.*

ARTIE, *uncomfortable:* She could've been one of the

big ones. A lady Biggie. Boy. Stardust. Handfuls
of it. All over her. Come on, boy . . . easy . . .
easy . . . Bill, that's enough.

BILLY: Do you have any tea bags?

ARTIE: You want a drink? Got the bourbon here—
the Jack Daniels—

BILLY: No. Tea bags. Two. One for each eye.

ARTIE, *puzzled:* Coming right up. . . . *He goes into
the kitchen and opens the cabinets.*

BILLY: Could you wet them? My future is all ashes,
Artie. In the morning, I'll fly back with Corrinna's body, fly back to L.A. and stay there. I can't
work. Not for a long, long time, if ever again. I
was supposed to go to Australia, but no . . . all
ashes. . . . *He puts one teabag over each eye.*
God, it's good to see you again, Artie.

ARTIE: Billy, you can't! You owe it—golly, Billy, the
world—Bunny and me—we fell out of our loge
seats—I'd be crazy if it wasn't for the laughs, for
the romance you bring. You can't let this death
stand in the way. Look what's happened to your
old buddy. I've become this Dreaming Boy. I
make all these Fatimas out of the future. Lourdes
and Fatima. All these shrines out of the future
and I keep crawling to them. Don't let that happen to you. Health. Health. You should make a
musical. Listen to this. *He goes to the piano and
sings and plays:*

Back together again,
Back together again . . .

BANANAS *appears in the bedroom doorway dressed in clothes that must have been very stylish and elegant ten years earlier.*

BILLY—*starts:* Georgina!!

ARTIE *stops playing.*

BANANAS: No, Billy . . .
BILLY—*stands up:* Oh God—for a minute I thought it was . . .
ARTIE: Don't she look terrific . . .
BILLY: Let me look at you. Turn around. *She does.* Jesus, didn't Georgina have good taste.
BANANAS, *turning:* I used to read *Vogue* on the newsstands to see what I'd be wearing in three years.
BILLY: Georgina took that dress right off her back and gave it to you. What a woman she was . . .
BANANAS: I put it on to make you happy, Billy.

BILLY *is crying again.*

ARTIE: Easy, Billy, easy . . .
BANANAS: It's a shame it's 1965. I'm like the best dressed woman of 1954.

BILLY, *starting to laugh and cheer up:* You got the best of them all, Artie. Hello, Bananas!

BANANAS: Sometimes I curse you for giving me that name, Billy.

BILLY: A little Italian girl. What else was I going to call her?

The LITTLE NUN *rushes in from the bedroom.*

LITTLE NUN: Mr. Shaughnessy! Quick—the bathtub —the shower—the hot water is steaming—running over—I can't turn it—there's nothing to turn—

ARTIE *runs into the bedroom. The* LITTLE NUN *looks at Billy.* BILLY *smiles at her. The* LITTLE NUN *runs into the bedroom.*

BANANAS: I did it to burn her.

BILLY: Burn who?

BANANAS: Burn her downstairs. Have the hot water run through the ceiling and give her blisters. He won't like her so much when she's covered with blisters. Hot water can do that. It's one of the nicest properties of hot water.

BILLY: Burn who???

BANANAS: Kate Smith!!

ARTIE, *running in from the bedroom to the kitchen:*

Wrench. Wrench. Screwdriver. *He rattles through drawers. Brightly to Billy:* God, don't seem possible. Twenty years ago. All started right on this block. Didn't we have some times? The Rainbow Room. Leon and Eddie's. I got the pictures right here.

The pictures are framed on the wall by the front door. BILLY *comes up to them.*

BILLY: Leon and Eddie's!
ARTIE, *indicating another picture:* The Village Barn.
BANANAS: The Village Barn. God, I loved the Village Barn.
ARTIE: It's closed, Bananas. Finished. Like you.
LITTLE NUN: Mr. Shaughnessy—please?

ARTIE *runs into the bedroom.*

Mr. Einhorn?
BILLY: Hello?
LITTLE NUN: I was an usher before I went in and your name always meant quality. *She runs into the bedroom.*
BILLY: Why— Thank you . . .
BANANAS: Help me, Billy? They're coming again to make me leave. Let me stay here? They'll listen to you. You see, they give me pills so I won't feel

anything. Now I don't mind not feeling anything
so long as I can remember feeling. You see? And
this apartment, you see, here, right here, I stand
in this corner and I remember laughing so hard.
Doubled up. At something Ronnie did. Artie
said. And I stand over here where I used to iron.
When I could iron, I'd iron right here, and even
then, the buttons, say, on button-down shirts
could make me sob, cry . . . and that window,
I'd stand right here and mix me a rye-and-ginger
Pick-Me-Up and watch the lights go on in the
Empire State Building and feel so tender . . .
unprotected. . . . I don't mind not feeling so
long as I can be in a place I remember feeling.
You get me? You get me? Don't look at me dead.
I'm no Georgina. I'm no Corrinna. Help me?
Help Ronnie?

BILLY: Ronnie's in jail.

BANANAS: I don't mind the bars. But he can't take
them. He's not strong like his mom. Come closer
to me? Don't let them hear. Oh, you kept your
mustache. *She strokes his eyebrows.* Nothing's
changed. *She sings:*

Should auld acquaintance be forgot . . .

ARTIE *comes out of the bedroom, soaking wet.*

ARTIE: Those are eyebrows, Bananas. Eyebrows. Come on, where is it? *He reaches behind Bananas' back and pulls the silver faucet handle from her clenched fist.* Billy, you see the wall I'm climbing. *He goes back into the bedroom with it.*

The LITTLE NUN *looks out into the living room.*

LITTLE NUN, *to Billy:* We never got introduced.
BILLY: Do I know you?

BANANAS *goes into the corner by the window.*

LITTLE NUN, *coming into the room:* No, but my two friends died with your friend today.
BILLY: I'm very sorry for you.
LITTLE NUN: No, it's all right. All they ever wanted to do was die and go to heaven and meet Jesus. The convent was very depressing. Pray a while. Scream a while. Well, they got their wish, so I'm happy.
BILLY: If your friends died with my friend, then that makes us—oh God! Bananas! That makes us all friends! You friends and me friends and we're all friends!
BANANAS: Help Ronnie. Help him. *She hands Billy the phone.*

BILLY, *on phone:* Operator—my friend the operator—get me person-to-person my friend General Buckley Revere in the Pentagon—202 LIncoln 5-5600.

ARTIE, *coming out of the bedroom:* No, Billy . . . no favors for Ronnie. The kid went AWOL. M.P.'s dragging him out of the house. You think I like that? *To Bananas:* That kid's your kid, Bananas. You got the crazy monopoly on all the screwball chromosomes in that kid.

BILLY: Buck? Bill.

ARTIE, *to Bananas:* Let him learn responsibility. Let him learn to be a man.

BILLY: Buck, just one favor: my godchild, Ron Shaughnessy. He's in the brig at Fort Dix. He wanted to see the Pope.

ARTIE, *to Bananas:* Billy and me served our country. You think Billy could call up generals like that if he wasn't a veteran! *To us:* I feel I got to apologize for the kid. . . . I tried to give him good strong things . . .

BILLY: Buck, has the Army lost such heart that it won't let a simple soldier get a glimpse of His Holiness . . .

The front door opens. BUNNY *enters. She looks swell and great and all the Webster Dictionary synonyms for terrific. She's all exclamation points: pink and white!!! She carries an open umbrella and a steaming casserole in her pot-holder-covered hands.*

BUNNY: Arthur, are you aware the Rains of Ranchipur are currently appearing on my ceiling?

ARTIE: Ssshhhhhhh. . . . *Indicating her pot:* Is that the veal and oranges?

BUNNY: That's right, Arthur. I'm downstairs making veal and oranges and what do I get from you? Boiling drips.

ARTIE: That's Billy. . . . Billy's here. *He takes the umbrella from her.*

BUNNY: Billy Einhorn here? And you didn't call me? Oh, Mr. Einhorn. *She steps into the room. She is beaming. She poses.* And that's why the word *Voilà* was invented. Excuse my rudeness. Hi, Artie. Hi, Bananas.

BILLY, *on phone:* Thank you, Buck. Yes, Yes, Terrific, Great. Talk to you tomorrow. Love ya. Thank you. *He hangs up.* Ronnie'll be all right. Buck will have him stationed in Rome with NATO. He'll do two weeks in the brig just to clear the records . . .

ARTIE: Then off to Rome? Won't that be interesting. And educational. Thank you, Billy. Thank you.

BILLY: Ronnie's lucky. Buck said everybody at Dix is skedded for Vietnam.

BUNNY: I wouldn't mind that. I love Chinese food.

ARTIE: That's the little girl from the steambath . . .

BILLY *notices Bunny. They laugh.*

BUNNY: Hi! I'm Bunny from right down below.

BILLY *kisses her hand.*

Oohhhh. . . . Artie, perhaps our grief-stricken visitor from Movieland would join us in a Snack à la Petite.

BILLY: No, no.

ARTIE: Come on, Bill.

BUNNY: Flying in on such short notice you must have all the starving people of Armenia in your tumtum, begging, "Feed me, feed me."

BILLY: Just a bite would be—

BANANAS—*comes down to us with Artie's scrapbook:* What they do is they make a scrapbook of all the things she can cook, then they paste them in the book—veal parmagina, eggplant meringue . . .

ARTIE *grabs it from her.*

Eughh . . .

ARTIE, *to Billy:* We make a scrapbook of all the things Bunny can cook, you see, then we paste them in the book.

They eat.

To us: I wish I had spoons enough for all of you.

BUNNY: Mr. Einhorn, I met your friend today before Hiroshima Mon Amour happened out there and all I got to say is I hope when I go I got two Sisters of Charity with me. I don't know your persuasion God-wise, but your friend Corrinna, whether she likes it or not, is right up there in Heaven tonight.

BILLY: Artie, you were right. We are what our women make us. Corrinna: how easily deaf becomes dead. It was her sickness that held us together. Health. Health. You were always healthy. You married a wonderful little Italian girl. You have a son. Where am I?

BUNNY: Deaf starlets. That's no life.

BILLY: So how come she's dead? Who blew her up?

BANANAS: It was on the eleven o'clock news.

BUNNY: Crying and explanations won't bring her back. Mr. Einhorn, if it took all this to get you here, I kiss the calendar for today. Grief puts erasers in my ears. My world is kept a beautiful place. Artie . . . I feel a song coming on.

ARTIE: How about a lovely tune, Bill, to go with that food. *He goes to the piano and plays.*

BUNNY—*opens the umbrella and does a dance with it, as she sings:*

Where is the devil in Evelyn?
What's it doing in Angela's eyes?
Evelyn is heavenly,
Angela's in a devil's disguise.
I know about the sin in Cynthia
And the hell in Helen of Troy,
But where is the devil in Evelyn?
What's it doing in Angela's eyes?
Oh boy!
What's it doing in Angela's eyes?

BILLY: My God!

ARTIE, *up from the piano:* What!

BILLY: Suddenly!

BANANAS: Was it the veal?

BILLY: I see future tenses! I see I can go on! Health! I have an extra ticket. Corrinna's ticket. For Australia.

ARTIE: God, Billy, I'd love to. I have all my music . . .

BILLY, *coming to Bunny:* Cook for me a while? Stay with me a while? In two hours a plane leaves from Kennedy and on to a whole new world. Los Angeles. We drop off Corrinna's body. Then on to Hawaii. Samoa. Nonstop to Melbourne. Someone who listens. That's what I need.

BUNNY: But my whole life is here . . .

Billy Einhorn and Bunny Flingus. *Background:* Artie Shaughnessy,
Bananas Shaughnessy, the Little Nun

·

BILLY: Chekhov was right. Work. Work. That's the only answer. All aboard??????

BUNNY: My my my my my my my . . .

ARTIE: Are you out of your head? Leaving in two hours? It takes about six months to get shots and passports—

BUNNY: Luckily two years ago I got shots and a passport in case I got luck with a raffle ticket to Paree. I'm in raffles all over the place.

ARTIE: Bunny—

BUNNY: Leave me alone, Arthur. I have to think. I don't know what to say. It's all so sudden.

The LITTLE NUN *comes out of the bedroom. She is in civvies. As a matter of fact, she has on one of Georgina's dresses, off the shoulder, all covered with artificial cherries. It is too big for her. She carries her wet habit.*

LITTLE NUN: I was catching a cold so I put on one of your dresses, Mrs. Shaughnessy. I have to go now. I want to thank you for the loveliest day I've ever had. You people are so lucky. You have so much. *She is near tears.* And your son is so cute. Maybe when I take my final vows I can cross my fingers and they won't count.

BILLY: How would you like to stay here?

ARTIE: Stay here?

BILLY: There'll be an empty apartment right down

below and you could come up and take care of Bananas. *He takes out his wallet and gives a number of hundred-dollar bills to the little nun.* How's this for a few months' salary?

ARTIE: What's all that money?

BILLY: Artie, don't send Bananas away. Love. That's all she needs.

BANANAS: It is? *The telephone rings. She answers it:* Yes? Yes? *To Artie, who is on his knees, trying to reason with Bunny:* It's the Zoo.

ARTIE: Tell them I'll call—what are they calling this late for?

BANANAS: The animals are all giving birth! Everything's having a baby. The leopards and the raccoons and the gorillas and the panthers and the . . .

ARTIE, *taking the phone:* Who is this? Al? Look, this is what you have to do. Heat the water. Lock the male elephants out. They get testy. The leopardess tends to eat her children. Watch her careful . . .

As he talks on the phone so we can't hear him, BUNNY *comes downstage and talks to us.*

BUNNY: The Pope saw my wish today. He looked me right in the eye and he winked. Hey! Smell—the bread is starting again and there's miracles in the

air! The Pope is flying back through the night-
time sky and all the planets fall back into place
and Orion the Hunter relaxes his bow . . . and
the gang war in Vietnam will be over and all
those crippled people can now stand up and
walk back to Toledo. And, Billy, in front of all
these people, I vow to you I'll be the best house-
keeper money can buy . . . and I'll cook for you
and clean and, who knows, maybe there'll be a
development. . . . And, Bananas, honey, when I
get to California, I'll send you some of my
clothes. I'll keep up Georgina's traditions. Sister,
here are the keys to my apartment downstairs.
You can write a book, *I Jump Over the Wall*,
and, Billy, you could film it.

ARTIE, *on phone:* Yes! I'll be right down. I'll be right
on the subway. Yes. *He hangs up.* I . . . have to
go to work. . . . Billy? Bun? Would you like to
come? See life starting? It's beautiful.

BUNNY, *in the kitchen:* Bananas, honey, could I have
this copper pot? I've always had my eye on this
pot.

BANANAS: Take it.

ARTIE: Listen, Bill.

BUNNY: Well, I'm packed.

ARTIE: I write songs, Bill. *He starts playing and
singing "Back Together Again."*

BANANAS, *to Billy, who is on his way out:* Thank you, Billy.

BILLY, *coming back and sitting alongside Artie:* Artie, can I tell you a secret?

ARTIE *stops playing.*

Do you know who I make my pictures for? Money? No. Prestige? No. I make them for you.

ARTIE: Me?

BILLY, *coming downstage:* I sit on the set and before every scene I say, "Would this make Artie laugh? Would this make Artie cry?"

ARTIE, *coming to Billy:* I could come on the set and tell you personal . . .

BILLY: Oh no, Artie. If I ever thought you and Bananas weren't here in Sunnyside, seeing my work, loving my work, I could never work again. You're my touch with reality.

He goes to Bananas: Bananas, do you know what the greatest talent in the world is? To be an audience. Anybody can create. But to be an audience . . . be an audience . . .

ARTIE—*Runs back to the piano; he sings desperately:*

I'm looking for something,
I've searched everywhere . . .

BUNNY: Artie, I mean this in the best possible sense:
You've been a wonderful neighbor.
BILLY, *to Artie:* I just saved your life.

They exit.
ARTIE *plays "Where is the Devil in Evelyn" hysterically, then runs out after them.*

ARTIE, *shouting:* Bill! Bill! I'm too old to be a young talent!!!

The LITTLE NUN *comes downstage.*

LITTLE NUN, *to us:* Life is this orchard and we walk beneath it and apples and grapes and cherries and mangoes all tumble down on us. Ask and you shall receive. I didn't even ask and look how much I have. Thank you. Thank you all.
  She kisses the television. A shrine . . . I wanted to be a Bride of Christ but I guess now I'm a young divorcee. I'll go downstairs and call up the convent. Good-bye. Thank you. *She wrings out her wet habit, then throws it up in the air and runs out.*

ARTIE *returns. He stands in the doorway.* BANANAS *sits on the edge of the armchair. She is se-*

rene and peaceful and beautiful. ARTIE *comes into the room slowly.*

BANANAS: I don't blame you for that lady, Artie. I really don't. But I'm going to be good to you now. Cooking. I didn't know you liked cooking. All these years and I didn't know you liked cooking. See, you can live with a person. . . . Oh God, Artie, it's like we're finally alone for the first time in our life. Like it's taken us eighteen years to get from the church to the hotel room and we're finally alone. I promise you I'll be different. I promise you . . .

She sits on her haunches like a little dog smiling for food as she did in Act One: Hello, Artie. *She barks. She sings:*

> Back together again,
> Back together again.
> Since we split up
> The skies we lit up
> Looked all bit up
> Like Fido chewed them,
> But they're
> Back together again.
> You can say you knew us when . . .

She begins barking. She crawls on all fours. She barks happily. She wags her behind. She licks Artie's hands. ARTIE *looks at her. He touches the piano and picks up his music. She rubs her face against his pants leg, nuzzling him. She whimpers happily. She barks. She sits up, begging, her hands tucked under her chin. Her hands swing out. She knocks the music out of his hands onto the floor. She rubs her face into Artie's legs. He pats her head. She is thrilled. He kneels down in front of her. He is crying. He touches her face. She beams. She licks his hand. He kisses her. He strokes her throat. He looks away. He holds her. He kisses her fully. She kisses him. He leans into her. As his hands go softly on her throat, she looks up at him with a beautiful smile as if she had always been waiting for this. He kisses her temples, her cheeks. His hands tighten around her throat. Their bodies blend as he moves on top of her. She smiles radiantly at him. He squeezes the breath out of her throat. She falls.*

Soft piano music plays.

The stage begins to change. Blue leaves begin to filter all over the room until it looks like ARTIE *is standing in a forest of leaves that are blue. A blue spotlight appears downstage and he steps into it. He is very happy and smiles at us.*

ARTIE: Hello. My name is Artie Shaughnessy and I'd
  like to thank you for that blue spot and to sing
  you some songs from the pen of. *He sings:*

> I'm here with bells on,
> Ringing out how I feel.
> I'll ring,
> I'll roar,
> I'll sing
> Encore!
> I'm here with bells on.
> Ring! Ring! Ring!

The stage is filled with blue leaves.

CURTAIN

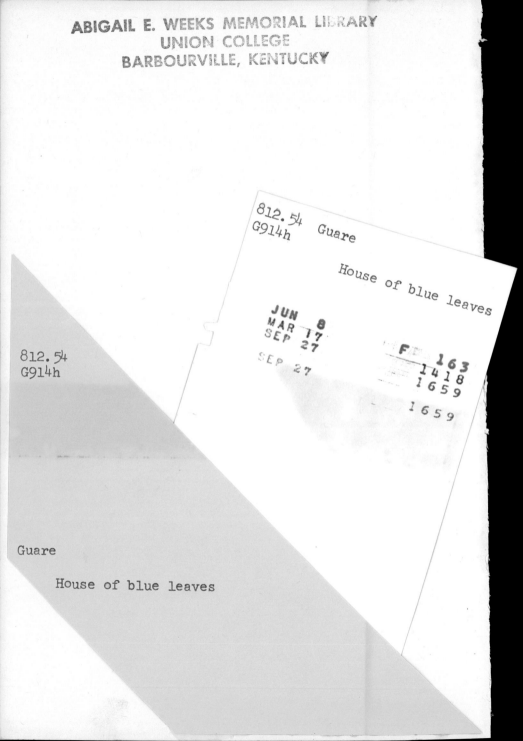